Secrets
of the
Cave

An Adventure of William and Anna

Bon Aqua, Tennessee
1915

BY
ANAH D. WEATHERS

615 - 385 - 2880 - 293-0270

Cover design and photograph
of the Big Spring Creek
by Luther Weathers

Secrets of the Cave

Published by Creative Services
Nashville, Tennessee

Copyright © 1999
under
ANNA AND WILLIAM/ TREASURES FROM THE PAST/BON AQUA 1915
by
Anah D. Weathers
1009 Paris Avenue, Nashville, TN 37204

Printed in the USA

Library of Congress Catalog Card Number: 00-109797

ISBN: 0-9702584-0-2

DEDICATED TO:

My mother, Mamie Davidson; my husband, Luther Weathers, Jr.; and my children and grandchildren whose love and support are always with me.

Contents

CHAPTER ONE

Bon Aqua School

Ten-year-old William Davis sat staring out the window of the little one-room schoolhouse. The pain he felt grew more intense as he remembered his pa hitting his ma the night before. His pa always yelled a lot and had slapped William and his two little sisters, but this was the first time he had ever hit his ma. "Why is Pa so mean to us?" he whispered to himself as he took a deep breath and closed his eyes.

Suddenly, William realized that it was his time to stand up and read aloud from his history book. He stood by his chair with his hands trembling and stumbled over the words in a low tone.

"Speak up! I can't hear you," he heard Miss Lois, his teacher, saying in a loud voice. William felt a tightness coming into his throat as he stood there. He tried to speak but could do nothing but stare at the page. It was almost like he was home again and his pa was shouting at him. Miss Lois glared at him through her gold-rimmed glasses, and he became aware that his face was getting red as he heard her saying, "Sit down and read silently. I'll spend time with you after school."

He quickly sat down and looked at his book, not even seeing it. He did not hear the other students as they continued to read. He was totally alone in his pain. "Stay after school? Now Pa will really be mad," he said under his breath, with the words "stay after school" echoing through his mind. "I hate reading," he mumbled, looking out the window to hide the tears running down his cheeks.

Suddenly, a small horse pulling a wagon load of corn came into William's view. He was trying to make his way up the steep hill of the wagon trail that ran in front of the schoolhouse. His coat was a deep chocolate brown, and he appeared to be very young, a pretty little horse. About halfway up the hill, he stopped to rest for a moment. The man, riding on the wagon load of corn, began whipping him with a long leather strap. The little horse struggled to go faster; but no matter how fast he went, the man continued to whip him.

William took a deep breath and let it out slowly as he closed his eyes to block the sight of the beating. After a few moments, he wiped his eyes, glanced down at his history book, and then up at the big clock that hung on the wall behind Miss Lois's desk. He was relieved when he saw that it was almost ten o'clock, recess time. He put his history book under his seat and laid his head in his arms, hoping that the little horse could slip away from the farmer. He reasoned that if the horse got away he could eat the hay that was piled at the back of the school building and drink water from the creek that ran to the right of the schoolhouse. The tightness in his throat subsided as he thought about his favorite spot, down the hill, near the water.

William sprang from his seat as he heard Miss Lois ringing the old cowbell for recess. He hurried to the door and ran down the steps ahead of the other students.

He was relieved when he glanced back over his

shoulder and saw Rupe, the tallest boy in the school, bending over the big wooden box by the door getting the basketball. If Rupe had not seen him maybe no one else had either, he thought as he ran down the hill toward his favorite place. Reaching the Big Spring Creek, he climbed up on a rock and looked all around for the little brown horse. He picked up a pebble, tossed it into the water, and watched the ripples circling and expanding outward as the small stone made its way to the bottom of the creek. Then he stretched out on the rock, listening to the sounds around him. His thoughts drifted back to the time he found this favorite spot.

It was about a year ago when Miss Lois decided to let the first-through-fourth-grade students play inside the school on Fridays. Up until that time, every day of the week she would follow her students to the door, lean over the wooden box, and pick up the softball. She would then walk down the steps and call the first, second, third, and fourth grade students to her side. If all were there, five girls and four boys would gather around her, eagerly anticipating a fun game of Pitch the Ball.

There were only nineteen students in the whole school. So, when the nine younger children were playing with the softball, more room was made for the ten older students to play with the basketball. But playing basketball at recess was not much fun for William, because Rupe and Mort constantly reached the brown box by the door and got the basketball before anyone else could get it. Then they threw it to each other. They would make shots into the hoop, while the shorter boys and girls ran around trying to get the ball from the bully and his friend. For this reason, William did not like recess. That is, not until Miss Lois started staying inside the building on Fridays. With her inside the school playing hopscotch on the old wooden floor with the younger boys and girls, William found it easy to slip away from the building without her seeing him. As William lay there on the big rock in his favorite place by the creek, he wished that every day could be Friday. That way, he would never have to play with Rupe and Mort, and he would always be able to come to this beautiful spot during recess time.

As William sat up, he looked all around for the horse but did not see him. Remembering the haystack, and hoping that the little animal had found his way there; he stood up on the rock, jumped down, and started up the hill toward the schoolhouse. Slipping to the back of the building, he stretched out in the big pile of hay near the chimney. His light-blue eyes filled with tears as he realized that, probably, the little horse was still with the cruel man.

His brown sandy hair and clothing blended with his surroundings so well that a bird landed beside him. Being very still, he watched the mother picking up grain from the straw and flying to the top of the chimney with a mouthful. William began to feel better as he heard baby birds chirping. Glancing above, he saw their tiny heads poking from the nest. He enjoyed watching the feeding process.

William moved only when he heard Miss Lois ringing the bell, signaling that recess was over. He got up from the pile of hay, ran to the front of the school-house, and walked into the building with the other students. He went quickly to his desk and opened his English book, hoping that no one had noticed that he was not with them at recess. He kept very quiet so that, maybe, Miss Lois would not call on him.

As William put his book away after class, he glanced out the window just in time to see Anna and her family walking up the hill along the wagon trail. She was tall and graceful and had ebony black skin like her papa's. He carried her twin brothers, one in each arm. Anna looked like she was about eleven years old. She walked on one side of her papa and her mama walked on the other. Her mama looked like an Indian princess. William noticed that Anna and her parents were talking and smiling as though they shared a great secret.

A warm feeling came over William as he watched the tall man smiling at the little boys. His arms were very big, and the boys were only about a year old, so it was with great ease that he carried them. He looked down at his sons and then at Anna's mama with the kindest smile William had ever seen.

William watched as they walked out of sight and wished that he could go with them instead of sitting in his seat at Bon Aqua School. He wondered why Anna wasn't there with the rest of the children. Everyone else he knew who was about her age was in school. "Why is she free to be with her family," he whispered to himself.

William's thoughts drifted back to the first time he saw Anna. It was then that Rupe had stood at the window pointing his finger while saying, in a mocking voice, "There goes Anna and her family. Wonder where they're going?" William had never liked Rupe, and he liked him even less when he made fun of people.

When the school day was over, all the students left for home except William. After about five minutes, Miss Lois walked over to his desk and said, "If you'll take that history book home with you and read your lesson tonight, you can leave." William was relieved as he put the book under his arm. He hurried out the door, past the basketball goal, and down the wagon trail toward home. He began to walk slowly as he neared the big colonial house that his pa had lived in since childhood.

William's grandpa had built the house many years before, and William, his ma and pa (whose names were Sarah and Oscar), and William's two little sisters lived there with Grandpa until he passed away. William had been told that when Oscar was a little boy, Grandpa made him work long hours on the farm. Many times he would not allow his little son to go to school but would demand that he stay home and help with the chores. This caused Oscar to make poor grades in school. One of the worst things that happened to Oscar was that when the other children were learning to read, his father made him stay home and work. With his father being so unkind to him, and with the burden of not being able to read, he felt very alone and rejected.

Years later, Grandpa realized that he had made many mistakes as a father when Oscar was growing up; so when William was born to Oscar and Sarah, he promised himself that he would try to be a better person. Gradually, he began to develop patience and understanding. He often took William horseback riding through the waters of the Big Spring Creek. Sometimes they took long walks together. William recalled the times when they stopped for the horse to drink the cool water, and then galloped through the valley and up the hill toward the road that led to Memphis. Grandpa had talked about he and William riding the horse all the way to the big city; but he became very ill and was unable to follow through with his plans. After months of being unable to walk, Grandpa died one wintery evening when the snow was on the ground.

Since his death, William had been very lonely. He missed his grandpa so much that it seemed his heart would almost break. Stopping at the gate that led up to his house, William turned and looked toward the wagon trail and thought of the first time Grandpa walked with him to Bon Aqua School. Their house was about a mile from the school; and when first grade started, William didn't want to go by himself. So Grandpa walked all the way holding William's hand. When school was over that day, his grandpa was waiting for him in front of the building. He walked with him every morning and evening until William felt comfortable walking by himself.

While opening the squeaking gate, William remembered his pa hitting his ma the night before. The tightness came into his throat again as he made his way up the steps and over to the front door. He stood there for a moment, listening. Soon he heard his two little sisters running through the house, laughing. He breathed a sigh of relief and opened the door. If his sisters were running and having fun, he knew that his pa was not at home because when he was there they always had to be quiet.

CHAPTER TWO

Recess

It was the third Friday in October. William stood by his seat at Bon Aqua School feeling very embarrassed because it was his time to read once again. His hands were shaky and sweaty, and he was unable to say even the first word.

"Sit down and read silently," he heard Miss Lois saying as he stood there trying to focus his eyes on the page. He slipped into his seat and stared at his history book. As soon as the other students were finished reading, he placed the book under his seat and glanced at the big clock on the wall.

William was glad that the clock was right behind Miss Lois's desk. That way, she would think that he was looking at her. As soon as she picked up the old cowbell, he was on alert and walked quickly from his seat. He ran down the steps, around the building, to the path that wound its way to the creek at the bottom of the hill. It felt good to be alone, and he began to listen to the sound of water rippling over the rocks. He did not go to his favorite place, but turned to his right and walked through the woods behind the schoolhouse.

As William rounded a curve, he saw someone. It was Anna. She was leaning against the big oak tree that grew in the middle of the forest. As he walked closer, he realized that she was reading a book. He felt his heart pounding. The more he tried to calm down the faster it seemed to beat.

When she saw him, she started to run, and he heard himself saying, "Please don't go. I've seen you walk by the schoolhouse and I know that your name is Anna."

She stopped and turned toward him.

"My name is William," he said.

Her timid smile let him see, for the first time, how beautiful she was. Curly ringlets softly accented her face. Her big brown eyes seemed to drink in everything around her. A light-blue ribbon firmly held her long black hair. They stood there looking at each other. He took a step toward her, and she said, "I must go." He watched as she turned and ran down the hill, through the woods, and out of sight.

Reluctantly, William walked slowly toward his favorite place by the creek wondering why Anna had run away. He wanted so much to talk with her. In his mind he could still see the light-blue ribbon holding her hair in place. He remembered that the ribbon was the same color as her long dress. When he reached the big rock, he sat for a while with the color of light-blue and the beauty of Anna in his thoughts. Suddenly realizing that recess might be over, he hurried up the hill and reached the playground just as the last student disappeared into the building. Running up the steps and closing the door behind him, he walked to his seat.

William thought about Anna all week, and even mentioned her name to his ma as they were talking one evening at the table.

"I've seen Anna and her family in the General Store, and I've heard that they own a farm somewhere near the school. Their last name is Gilbert, and they seem to be good people," Ma said as she sliced William a piece of jam cake.

William and Ma talked for a long time that evening.

The following Friday morning during his history class at Bon Aqua School, William could hardly wait until recess. As Miss Lois rang the bell, he got up from his seat, hurried to the door and walked quickly down the steps. He could hear the basketball bouncing on the hard brown earth as he ran to the back of the building and down the path toward the old oak tree. William, hoping that his absence would not be noticed by Miss Lois or the children, ran very fast. He stopped suddenly when he saw Anna.

She did not see him. She had fallen asleep after eating the ham and biscuit her mama had prepared. William stood looking at her. "Anna," he said softly. Startled, she sat up. "Why is it that you don't go to school?" he asked. Anna dropped her head and would not look at him. Sensing that she was experiencing feelings similar to the ones he often felt when his pa shouted at him, William reasoned to himself, "Her pa hates her like my pa hates me. This can't be true," he thought, remembering the happy family walking by the school. He looked at Anna as she sat there with her head bowed, and wondered what was making her so sad. He walked over and sat down at the base of the tree beside her. He had never been so close! This time his heart was not pounding. His only thought was to make her feel better. In a gentle voice, he asked again, "Why don't you go to school?"

Anna said softly, "You don't know, do you, William?"

William had no idea what she meant. He leaned forward waiting for her to continue.

"I can't go to Bon Aqua School because my skin isn't white," she said.

It was hard for William to understand why that would make her so sad. He hated going to school. He always had trouble reading and he didn't like the way Miss Lois looked at him through those glasses. And he was sure that Anna wouldn't like being in the same room with Mort and Rupe.

Anna picked up the tin bucket and book, and with one sweeping move was on her feet, running down the path, deep into the forest. William started to follow, but instead called her name. With the sound of his voice echoing through the woods, he realized that someone on the playground might hear him. If Miss Lois found out that he had slipped away from school, he would be in serious trouble. Especially if she told his pa.

William slowly made his way to his favorite place by the Big Spring Creek. He watched the butterflies as they circled over the water. They were bright yellow with black trim around their wings. They were bigger than most he had seen. He listened to the birds singing as he leaned back against his favorite rock and closed his eyes. The sunlight filtering through the trees felt good as he rested there for a while.

He returned to the school and walked to the playground where the shorter boys and girls were trying to get the basketball from Mort and Rupe. While standing there watching, he hoped that no one was aware that he had just walked up. He was relieved when the bell rang and the children walked toward the school, not noticing him. It was only then that he knew his absence had not been detected.

One week later, things did not go so smoothly. As William ran down the steps and around the side of the building at recess time, Miss Lois pushed up one of the windows.

"Where are you going, William?" she shouted as she glared at him through those glasses.

William stopped instantly and turned toward her. With an unpleasant look she motioned for him to come inside. Slowly he walked to the front of the building and up the steps. She met him at the door and snapped, "Where were you going?"

William dropped his head and mumbled, "For a walk in the woods."

"Not during school time," she blurted out as she shoved her hands deep into the pockets of her long gray dress. "Go to your desk and study your history lesson. If this happens again, I'll tell your ma and pa."

That tightness came into William's throat again. He opened his history book but was unable to keep his mind on the lesson. He tried to read, but the more he tried the more he thought about Anna and the fact that he might never see her again.

This was the beginning of a very hard time for William. He often wished that he could be free to walk through the woods and wade in the water. Sometimes tears came into his eyes as he looked out the window of the little one-room schoolhouse.

The warm days turned to windy days and then to cold days. From December to March, the cold winds blew so hard that, sometimes, the students had to pull their chairs close to the fireplace in order to stay warm as Miss Lois taught their classes.

On winter evenings, when William's pa was not there, he would sit with his ma at the kitchen table and talk. He liked talking with her. She was always able to say just the right thing to make him feel better. The warmth of her smile and the warmth he felt from the little cook stove made an inviting place. It was cozy and peaceful when Pa was not around. Sometimes, William wished that he would not return, but that thought always made him feel guilty.

He usually enjoyed helping his ma with the chores. They took turns milking the cow, feeding the chickens, and gathering the eggs. And the horse—he always liked feeding the horse. William was on his way to the barn one morning with his milk bucket when he noticed that the flowers had begun to poke their heads through the moist ground. "Yeah, it won't be long until spring," he said under his breath. "Planting time, I love planting time."

He wondered where Anna was and what she was doing. He hoped that she and her family would walk by the school again, now that the days were getting warmer.

Finally, school was out and it was time for all the children to help their parents in the fields. Planting corn was one thing William liked to do, even with his pa. He would drop the grains of corn in the long rows while his pa followed with the horse, plowing the rich soil over the seed. About two weeks later, they would walk to the cornfield to see if the corn was coming up.

Watching the tiny green sprouts as they pushed their way through the soil was exciting for William. Sometimes he went to the cornfield alone just to see how much the corn had grown. When there was a sunny day after a slow rain, it grew very fast. Since he could not actually see it getting taller, he wondered if it might do most of its growing at night. He wondered about many things as he enjoyed the planting time on his pa's farm.

Summer was different for William. He hated it. Summer meant he had to chop weeds from the corn. He always grew very tired with the hot sun beaming down on his shoulders.

CHAPTER THREE

July Fourth Celebration - 1915

William sat on the steps of the General Store and watched the men, women, boys, and girls arriving by train. They came from all over the United States to visit the quaint little village of Bon Aqua, so that they could stay at the lavish Bon Aqua Springs Resort. They stepped down from the train and climbed into awaiting horse-drawn carriages. William had heard that the travelers were carried down a winding road, through enchanted gardens, past virgin springs, and on to the lovely resort. The excitement of the happy people made William long for the day when he could slip inside one of the carriages and go with them.

He had asked his pa ever since he was eight years old if he could go to Bon Aqua Springs; but he was never allowed to go, not even to the big July Fourth Celebration. William decided that he would ask one more time. Maybe now that he was almost eleven, he could go. William was excited as he left the General Store. He felt confident that his pa would say "yes".

That evening, William heard the car pulling into the shed. He ran outside, walked up to Pa as he got out of the car, and said, "Can I go to Bon Aqua Springs Resort tomorrow for the July Fourth Celebration?"

"No, William! Don't bother me, I'm in a hurry."

"Why, Pa? Why can't I go? I've never been! All the other children from school will be there," William pleaded as he followed him through the yard. Pa said nothing, but quickly walked into the house and slammed the kitchen door behind him.

William stayed outside for a long time and then went around the house and slipped in the front way. He walked into his room and lay on the bed thinking about how much fun he would have if Pa would just let him go. He went to bed late that night still hoping that he would get a positive answer.

As Pa came into the kitchen the next morning, William said, "Please, Pa, please let me go to Bon Aqua Springs today to the July Fourth Celebration."

"No, I've told you my last time! You're not going to any kind of celebration when there's so much work to be done on this farm! And you had better have that cornfield chopped clean when I return," he shouted angrily as he stomped out the back door.

A big lump rose up in William's throat as he heard his pa backing the car out of the driveway. He had wanted so much to go, and now all hope was gone. He knew that he would have to stay home and chop Johnsongrass and other weeds from the cornfield while everyone else had fun at Bon Aqua Springs. William choked back the tears as his ma came into the kitchen. He did not want her to see him crying for he was now past ten years old, but he wanted more than anything else to go to the celebration.

"I'll take care of feeding the chickens, the horse, and milking and feeding the cow," Ma said as she placed a bowl of oatmeal in front of William. "That way, maybe you'll be able to chop all the weeds from the corn before your pa returns."

William nodded his head as he tried to swallow a mouthful of oatmeal. He tried hard to make it go down. There was a lot of pain in his throat and he felt like he was going to choke. He had felt this way many times, but this time it was worse. He forced down a swallow of milk and said, "Thank you, Ma."

She quickly wrapped scrambled eggs on a biscuit for him, placed it in a tin bucket, and made sure that the lid was pushed down tightly. She poured water into a second bucket and handed both to William.

"Thank you, Ma," he said swallowing the tears and walking out the back door. As he passed, she touched him on the shoulder and said, "I'm proud of you, William."

Tears filled his eyes as he walked down the steps, holding both buckets by the wire handles in one hand. With the other hand, he picked up the hoe that was leaning against the house and walked toward the cornfield.

William chopped weeds all morning until his back began to ache. About ten thirty, he sat down on the soft soil between two rows of corn for a break. As he stretched out on the moist ground, he felt a cool breeze blowing across his body. While lying there enjoying the brief moment of rest, he thought about his ma and felt thankful that he was the oldest child in the family. She depended on him to help her with his two younger sisters, Mary and Rose, and this made him feel good. It comforted him to feel her support, especially when Pa was shouting at him. He wondered again why Pa was so mean to them, as he took a deep breath and closed his eyes.

William could have easily gone to sleep on the cool moist ground, but the sound of horses pulling a wagon caused him to sit up. "Another family going to Bon Aqua Springs Resort," he said under his breath as that lonely feeling came over him again. Tears ran down his cheeks as he thought about having to stay there and chop weeds while everyone else was having fun at the celebration.

William listened to the horses' hooves on the dirt road as they passed the big cornfield. He heard laughter coming from the wagon and crouched closer to the ground so he would not be seen. He felt ashamed that he had to stay home and work.

He lay there on the ground until the sound of the wagon was past the rows of corn where he was hiding. After a moment, he raised his head and peered through the weeds just in time to see the tall dark man on the front seat of the wagon give the lady sitting next to him a little kiss on the cheek. On the seat behind the couple was a girl sitting between two little boys. Suddenly, William realized who was on the wagon. "That's Anna's family!" he almost shouted aloud. But he controlled himself and let the realization float through his mind, silently. He stayed very still and watched.

The boys were now about two years old. William could tell that they were playing some kind of game with their hands. The seats they were sitting on were made of big pieces of wood like the ones William had seen on wagon trains. Behind the second seat was a blanket of hay with soft pillows where the children could lie down and sleep if they grew tired. William watched the happy family until the wagon was out of sight. He wished that his ma and pa and little sisters could ride together on a wagon like that.

He sank back down on the ground and listened to the wheels squeaking until they grew faint in the distance. Then, remembering how sad Anna was the last time they talked, he felt better knowing that she was going to Bon Aqua Springs for the big celebration. "Maybe having fun with all the others will help her not be so sad," he thought, as he took the lid off the tin bucket and began eating the scrambled eggs and biscuit his ma had prepared. He lay down on the ground and rested a while longer. Then he stood up and drank water from the other bucket. Putting lids on both, he picked up his hoe and started chopping weeds again.

The day wore on, and the sun made William very hot. Drops of sweat fell from his face, and he longed for a cool breath of air to cool his body. But he knew that he had to keep busy if he were to get his day's work done. He chopped weeds from the field for the rest of the day, and he kept thinking about Anna.

Finishing the last row of corn, he made his way through the tall stalks to the back of the house, hoping that his pa's 1915 Ford would not be in the shed. If the car was gone, his pa would be gone, too. If the car was there, his pa would be there, and he really didn't want to see him.

William was in luck. The shed stood silent, empty as a peanut shell that had just been opened. He propped the hoe against the side of the house and ran up the steps.

"Ma, I'm home. Finally finished hoeing that cornfield," he said loudly, as he walked through the kitchen and into his ma's bedroom.

She put her finger to her lips with a shhh . . . as she rocked two-year-old Rose in the big rocker by the window. Mary, his four-year-old sister, was already asleep on the bed in the corner of the room.

William walked back into the kitchen and drank a dipper full of water from the wooden bucket on the washstand. He had just stretched out on the kitchen floor to rest when Ma walked into the room and sat down at the table. He loved it when she would sit and talk while Pa was gone and the girls were asleep. It was her time to relax and share her thoughts with him. William got up and poured water from the bucket into a pan. He washed his hands and splashed water on his face. He dried his face and hands with a small towel as he sat down in the chair across from Ma. Then, she got up and poured William a bowl of potato soup, sprinkled cheese on it, and placed it in front of him, with a portion of her delicious cornbread. He eagerly ate, and washed it all down with a large glass of milk.

"That was good, Ma!" She smiled at him gently. "Saw Anna and her family going to the July Fourth Celebration in their wagon today."

"I didn't know they worked there."

"They don't! They were going for a fun day. They do a lot of things together," he said with his eyes downcast.

A serious look came over Ma's face as she leaned toward him saying, "Are you sure?"

Returning her serious look, William said, "That's where everyone was going today."

"William, Anna's family and all other people with dark skin are not allowed to go to Bon Aqua Springs Resort for any kind of celebration."

"What! Anna can't go to the celebration?"

"It's very unfair," Ma said. "There are many things in this world that are wrong."

"But Ma," William interrupted, "Anna lives in Bon Aqua. Everyone who lives here should be able to go. She can't even go to school!" His voice trembled, and he laid his head in his arms on the table as tears ran down his face. The tears would not stop. He thought of the many times he had wanted to go to the celebration, and his pa would not let him.

Ma wiped the moisture from her eyes. "Life is so full of pain," she thought as she sat there with William. She understood how he felt for she had experienced rejection through the years the same as he.

William wept silently until he fell asleep at the table. He awoke sometime later, with his ma helping him up from his chair. He leaned on her shoulder as she led him into his room. He was exhausted from his day of work in the sun, but he felt a little better since the tears had washed away some of the pain.

"Ma, I'd like to go for a long walk tomorrow morning," he said as he sat down on the edge of his bed. "Maybe, if I follow the path behind Bon Aqua School, I'll find Anna's house and be able to talk with her."

"It's okay with me, William, but be home by ten o'clock. Your pa will be gone until way into the night and won't start working on the farm until late tomorrow morning. If you are not here when he is ready to go to the field, you know how angry he'll be."

Ma stood in the doorway for a moment, then turned and walked back into the kitchen. She returned with a big wash pan half full of warm water, a bar of soap, and a clean towel and washcloth. She laid the soap, towel, and washcloth beside the pan on the wash stand. "Wash yourself good before crawling between those clean sheets tonight," she said as she walked from William's room.

William got up from the bed, bathed, and put his night clothes on. He felt better as he lay on his pillow, but there was still pain at the thought of Anna not being able to go to the celebration. He breathed deeply as he remembered the sadness on her face when she told him that she couldn't go to Bon Aqua School because her skin wasn't white.

In William's mind he could see Anna asleep by the big oak tree. He felt he could almost reach out and touch the light-blue ribbon that held her long black hair from her face. He drifted off to sleep, comforted by the thought of seeing her again.

CHAPTER FOUR

Sounds of the Farm

William awoke early to the sound of birds singing. He rolled out of bed, ate his breakfast, and was on his way toward Bon Aqua School by seven o'clock. He was not sure where Anna lived; but with the early start, he would surely find her before time to return.

Reaching the playground area in front of the school, he maneuvered around as though he were bouncing a basketball and then gestured as though he were throwing it into the hoop. It felt good! He had never been able to get the ball from Mort and Rupe at recess time, and had wanted so much to throw a ball through that hoop. He hoped that someday he would be able to get a basketball and play as long as he wanted.

There was excitement in the air as William ran down the path toward the old oak tree. He hoped that the path would take him right to Anna's house. When he came to the creek at the bottom of the hill, he sat down on a big rock and started to take off his shoes and socks and wade across. But then he noticed that several large stones had been placed across the water to the left of him. Thinking that was a perfect place to cross, he got up and walked to the water's edge. It was fun, jumping from one rock to the other. He didn't care if he did get his shoes wet. He was sure that they would dry before he returned home.

Safely on the other side of the creek, William noticed that the path led in two directions, one up over the hill and the other down the creek to the right. He stayed close to the creek. It was fun running down the path, watching the fish darting here and there. The water was clear. Bubbles found their way to the surface, and the early morning sun made them glisten as though they were diamonds. Now and then William saw a small fish swimming downstream. He wished that he had some of Ma's biscuits. Then he could throw the crumbs and maybe they would swim closer to the bank. He felt a bond, as though he and the fish were on a great adventure.

After walking about one-half mile, William heard a cow mooing in the distance. He walked a few more steps and realized that the sound was coming from his left. Seeing a path, he followed it halfway up the hill to a large clearing. A small barn stood beside the wooded area. William walked quietly to it's side, listening. He heard milk from a cow hitting the bottom of a tin bucket. He knew that sound for he had been milking cows since he was eight years old. His heart pounded. Maybe, just maybe, Anna was inside.

He slipped to the front of the barn. The sound of milk hitting the bottom of a tin bucket changed to milk hitting milk. "Whoever is milking that cow must have strong hands," William thought as he listened to the milk going into the bucket very fast. It sounded to him as though the person was milking with both hands. His grandpa used to milk that way before he passed away. William remembered him saying that when you milk with both hands you fill up the bucket in half the time.

William walked behind the barn door, listening. He watched while three kittens rounded the corner of the barn and ran to the stable where the cow was being milked. As William stood very still, the sound of milk hitting a tin pan reached his ears, then the sound of kittens lapping up milk. He loved the sounds of the farm, the birds singing, the bees buzzing, the soft wind blowing the hay. He could tell that it was hay by the aroma. He took a deep breath and leaned back against the barn.

The stable door flew open and out came the cow. A tall black man, with broad shoulders, walked close behind carrying a bucket full of milk. Excitement rushed through William for he recognized the man. He was Anna's papa. He carried the milk inside the little log cabin nestled in the trees about one-hundred-fifty feet from the barn. After a few moments, William started to walk up on the porch and knock, but he decided to wait and see if Anna would come outside instead.

Suddenly William heard the door open. Looking toward the cabin, he saw Anna standing in the doorway with an apron full of shelled corn. She walked across the porch, down the steps, and over to the chicken house. She held the corners of her apron up so she would not spill the corn, and with the other hand she opened the chicken house door. Chickens flew out the open door in all directions. At least three flew over Anna's head while others flew around her. A few waddled out as though they were too old to fly.

Anna walked a few feet from the chicken house and began throwing the corn out of her apron. Some of the chickens caught the grain in midair, while others ate from the ground.

After shaking her apron clean, Anna started walking toward the cow. A big collie ran to her side, and the two escorted the Jersey to the pasture behind the barn. The collie made a quick turn and the big animal went through the gate. "That's a good girl, Lady," Anna said, as she patted her brown and white pet on the head. Lady's ears perked up, as Anna closed the squeaking gate, and she looked up as if to say, "Stay with me for a while." Anna sat down on the ground, and the big collie stretched out beside her favorite friend, laying her head in Anna's lap. Both listened to sounds coming from the pasture as the cow grazed the long shoots of tender grass.

Insects, jumping to safety as the big animal made her way closer to the fence, caused Anna and Lady to jump up at the same time. Lady started chasing a grasshopper that had just escaped the jaws of the big Jersey. "Leave that grasshopper alone," Anna shouted as she walked toward the barn, a little disappointed in Lady's pursuit.

Anna climbed up on the wagon that was in the hallway of the old structure and sat on the front seat where her mama and papa always sat when they were going to the General Store, to grandma and grandpa's house, or to church. Anna leaned back on the seat and dreamed of traveling to places she had read about, like Memphis and Nashville. And maybe someday she might even go to Richmond or New Orleans. She was thinking about the cities her grandpa had traveled to when he was in the war, just as William slipped to the back of the barn and called her name.

Startled, Anna jumped from the wagon.

William felt his heart pounding as he stood there staring at her.

Her questioning eyes met his as she asked, "What are you doing here?"

"I saw you yesterday in the wagon as you passed the cornfield where I was chopping weeds. I thought you were going to the celebration at Bon Aqua Springs."

"We were coming from my Grandma's and Grandpa's house. Did you go?" she asked.

William looked toward the ground as he said in a low tone, "No, my pa wouldn't let me."

"I know how you feel," she said. "When I was younger, I wanted to go to the celebration, too. Now, that I'm older, I know there are more important things."

"Like what?"

"Wait here! I'll be right back," she said as she turned and ran to the log cabin. Moments later she returned carrying a stack of newspapers in her arms. "Let's go down by the creek. There's a big rock with tree roots growing around it. We can sit there and look at the papers." As they walked down the hill she mentioned that her mama told her to return within an hour.

When they got to the creek, William glanced at the sun and determined that when it positioned itself behind the tree to the right, her hour would be up. He was good at determining what time of day it was by looking at the position of the sun. He learned that from working in the cornfield.

The large flat rock made a good table. Anna laid the newspapers on it and sat down on one of the roots that ran along its side. Looking up and surveying her surroundings, she said, "This is a great place. I've been here many times."

William leaned against the tree while Anna turned the pages of the newspapers.

"Do you know about Helen Keller?" she asked.

"No, who is she?"

Anna picked up one of the papers and read that Helen Keller was born in Tuscumbia, Alabama, in 1880. The article went on to say that at the age of two years old she had an illness that caused her to lose her sight and hearing. Anna laid the paper down as she continued to talk about Helen. "Miss Anne Sullivan taught her to read braille. She also taught her how to communicate by touch. Later Helen learned to use a special typewriter and wrote her life's story." Anna whispered excitedly as she looked up at William, "My parents gave me her book for my birthday."

William did not respond but stared at the papers laying on the big rock.

"What's wrong?" Anna asked.

"You read so well. I wish I could read half that good."

"My parents taught me. Mama helped me with my ABCs and numbers during the day and Papa helped me read when he returned from the fields at night. In the winter time when Papa didn't have to work so hard, we sat by the fireplace. Mamma would bring our wire popcorn popper into the big room and Papa would hold it by its long handle and shake the corn over the flames in the fireplace.

It was always fun to count the corn as it began to pop. Then it would start popping so fast that even Papa couldn't keep up with the counting. I always had fun learning with him. He's the one who taught Mama how to read.

"Mama spoke Cherokee and could write the Indian sign language but didn't know much about English until she met my pa. They met when she was very young, about fourteen, I think. Papa is a lot older than mama. He taught her how to read and write English. Then she taught him Cherokee and some of the sign language."

"How did your papa learn to read?" William asked.

"When he was a little boy his parents were slaves. They were brought to America on a slave boat and had to work very hard. While his mama and papa worked on the farms, he listened to the white children as they read their story books. They passed them on to him when they were finished with them. He said that he has always liked to read. I do too. I guess I get that from him."

"You know a lot about your mama and papa. All I know about mine is that my ma is good to me, but it's almost like my pa hates me." Then he asked, looking intently at Anna, "What could be more important than going to the celebration?"

"Reading about faraway places and learning about the people who live in those places," Anna said as she turned to another portion of the paper. "Listen to this!" She read about Orville and Wilbur Wright and how they flew their first air ship at Kitty Hawk, North Carolina. "That made believers out of a lot of people," she said smiling.

Anna noticed that William looked very sad, so she pulled a paper from the bottom of the stack and read to him about members of an automobile club being arrested for breaking the speed limit. The drivers were going thirty miles per hour in an eight-mile-an-hour zone. Anna continued to read about the Justice of the Peace giving the drivers of the cars speed tickets.

William looked at the paper, "Wow, thirty miles an hour. That's fast! I see what you mean, Anna. Maybe reading can be fun. I wish I could read as good as you."

"You can," Anna said convincingly. "When I first started reading I was very slow. The more I read, the faster I got. It's a little like cars. At first they would only go a few miles an hour. Now they will go thirty. If they keep getting better, they'll be going sixty miles an hour."

"You're right! Can I borrow the paper that tells about the car race?"

"Sure!" she said.

As William sat down beside her, he noticed that the sun was almost to the tree that marked Anna's hour. "What other fun things do you know about?" he asked.

"My papa has a map of the world. It shows the oceans and the land between them. I like to look at the map of Africa when he tells me stories about my grandpa and grandma before they became slaves.

"Another thing that's fun is to look for Indian relics. Indian people lived all through these hills many years ago. My papa has found many arrowheads, and I have about fifteen of my own.

We found most of them in the creek bed. The creek runs into a cave and then goes under the ground. It comes out about fifty feet downstream. That's where my papa found most of his collection. Inside the cave there are stone steps going up from the creek. It's very dark when you first enter but when you go into the second room there's a big hole in the ceiling. The sunlight shines in so you can sit there and read and pretend that you are in an Indian school. It's so much fun, knowing that Indian children used to learn Cherokee in the cave school."

"How do you know that it was a school?"

"There are drawings on the rock wall where they did their lessons."

"Will you take me there sometime?"

"Yes, we'll go to the cave the next time you come."

William, glancing at the sun, got up from the tree trunk and started picking up the newspapers. "Your hour is almost up," he said. "I'll walk with you up the hill, through the woods, to your papa's barn. Have you read other stories in these newspapers?"

"I've read almost all of them. Some are funny and others are very sad. About fifty-five years ago the North and South soldiers were fighting each other all through Tennessee and other states. My grandpa slipped away and became one of the Northern soldiers. The North won the war and all the slaves were set free. If it had not been for my grandpa and others fighting for our freedom, we would not be able to live on our little farm. We would still be slaves."

"I know you're proud of your grandpa," William said as they made their way up the hill. Reaching the barn, he handed her all the newspapers except the one about the thirty-mile-an-hour race. "Thank you for letting me borrow this. I'll bring it back the next time I come."

"Can you come Sunday? As soon as dinner is over, Papa, Lady, and I usually go to the creek. So come after dinner next Sunday and I'll show you the cave."

William touched her hand as he said, "Thank you for telling me about the cave. I'll bring your paper back Sunday."

He turned and ran down the hill. He didn't want to leave. She was the nicest person he had ever talked to, and she was pretty, too. He ran fast so that leaving wouldn't be so hard. He stopped when he got to the creek so he could rest a moment. Standing there, he became aware of the sounds of the forest and the water rippling over the rocks. He folded the page from the newspaper Anna had loaned him, and put it in his pant's pocket. Then he pulled off his shoes and socks and waded up the creek, glancing now and then for Indian relics.

When he reached the place where he had crossed the creek earlier, he turned up the path that led to Bon Aqua School. Halfway up the hill toward the playground, he remembered how sad he was at recess when Mort and Rupe would not let him play ball. Reaching the school, he sat on the steps and looked at the basketball goal. "Maybe, someday, I'll be tall enough to play," he thought, as he wiped the dust from his feet. He put on his socks and shoes and hurried home.

CHAPTER FIVE

Good Feelings

William slipped in the back door, took a dipper of cold water from the bucket, and drank every drop of it. He lay down in the middle of the kitchen floor, thinking about Anna and all the things she had talked about. A good feeling came over him as he drifted off to sleep. He slept only a few minutes, and then was awakened by his pa ready to go to the field.

William worked very hard that week. He even tried to milk his pa's cow with both hands. But his wrists grew so tired he had to rest one hand while he milked with the other. Early one morning, he heard Pa in the shed starting the Ford. William jumped out of bed, dressed quickly, and by the time his pa's car reached the wagon trail, William was on his way to the barn. He called his two cats as he walked toward the cow's stable. He had a tin bucket in one hand and a pan in the other. The cats lapped up the warm milk as William forced it from the cow into the pan. It was fun watching them. Finishing the milking, he wondered if Pa would notice that some of it was missing. "Cats need milk, too," he said in a low voice as he smiled and picked up the less-than-full bucket.

"Ma, I've finished milking," he called as he entered the kitchen. He put the milk on the side table. The smell of breakfast, especially bacon frying on the wood-burning stove, made him eager to sit down at the kitchen table. But first he got a dipper of water and poured it into the pan. Then, with both hands, he splashed cool water on his face and washed his hands and arms all the way to his elbows. He sat down at the table, still drying his face and hands. While laying the towel down and stretching, he realized that he felt a lot taller.

Ma put a plate of bacon, eggs, and hot biscuits on the table in front of him. "Yum! This sure smells good," he said as he put a spoonful of peach preserves on his plate. He ate eagerly, then sat for a long time at the kitchen table talking with Ma. He told her about his visit with Anna and how she had read about Helen Keller. Then he talked about Orville and Wilbur Wright who were able to fly through the air on their aircraft. He pulled the newspaper from his pocket and handed it to her.

"Read this! I borrowed it from Anna," he said.

After reading the newspaper article, Ma said, "Thirty miles an hour. That's very fast!"

They sat for a long time that morning, laughing and talking about many things. After a while, two-year-old Rose and four-year-old Mary walked into the kitchen. They had been awakened by William and Ma laughing and wanted to join them. Ma picked up Rose, and Mary climbed up on the bench and scooted down close to William.

William continued talking about the car that

would go thirty miles an hour and the aircraft that would carry men through the air. He told Rose and Mary all about them as his ma looked on smiling.

CHAPTER SIX

Horseback Riding

As William awoke, he was thankful that it was Sunday. His pa always slept late on Sundays, then left in the Ford, and usually did not return until late that night. When Pa was not there, Ma would help William with the chores. Then she would let him go to the creek, horseback ride, or do other fun things like play games inside the house with his two little sisters. He especially liked playing inside when the weather was bad if his pa was not there. When his pa was home, they always had to be very quiet or he would start yelling at them.

After Sunday dinner, William told Ma that he wanted to ride Good Boy to Anna's house.

"Fine," she said. "Make sure you're home for supper." (In those days "dinner" was eaten in the middle of the day and the evening meal was called supper. Supper usually consisted of leftovers from dinner or maybe just a glass of cold milk with corn bread. At William's house the milk was kept cold by sealing it in tin buckets and placing the buckets in the spring of water at the bottom of the hill.)

"I'm glad you're horseback riding today. Good Boy needs some exercise," Ma said as she walked to the barn with William. She lifted the bridle and saddle from a rack inside the barn, then opened the stable door on the right. A brown horse, with a white patch on his nose, stood eating hay. She lifted the bridle, placed it around the horse's neck, and put the saddle on his back, while saying, "Good Boy, you are a good boy." Then she led the animal out of the barn and helped William climb up on the saddle.

"Thanks, Ma. I'll be home before supper time," he said as he straightened himself on Good Boy's back. William rode across the yard, turned, and waved to Ma before his horse galloped out of sight. This was the first time he had ridden horseback since school was out. He had great fun! He promised Good Boy that he would ride him more often.

When William reached the school yard, instead of turning into the playground area, he stayed on the wagon trail and went down the hill where it ran across the creek. His horse stopped and drank some of the cool fresh water before crossing, then galloped through the valley by the stream. Suddenly, they came to a stop as a rabbit ran in front of them. The horse sniffed the area, made a funny noise, and continued on the path as the rabbit ran into the bushes. The trail wound its way up the hill and continued along a plateau for about a mile, then went downhill a little bit and divided, with one part going up to the left and the other continuing down through the woods. Seeing Anna's log cabin in the distance, William breathed a sigh of relief. As he turned down the path that led to her pa's farm, he glanced back over his shoulder at the wagon trail that curved up the hill, thinking how much fun it would be to travel it all the way to Memphis.

He began to feel uneasy as he rode toward the barn. He had seen Anna's family but had never talked to any of them, except Anna. He began to feel better when he remembered how nice she was. He looked further down the hill through the woods toward the creek and wondered if Good Boy could walk down such a steep hill. He brought him to a stop at the barn and climbed down off the saddle and stood for a few moments rubbing him on the back. Then, tying him to the gate post, he walked over to the log cabin, up the steps, and knocked on the door.

He took a deep breath as Anna's papa appeared in the doorway.

"I'm horseback riding and wondered if Anna could ride, too," he said quickly as he took another deep breath.

"We were talking about going for a walk," the tall man said looking down at William.

William felt very small and didn't know what to say so he just stood there.

Anna came to the door and said, "Hi, William, this is my papa. His name is John Gilbert."

"Hi, Mr. Gilbert."

With a pleading look, Anna continued, "I want to go horseback riding, Papa. That's more fun than walking."

"Well, let's see what we can do about this," Mr. Gilbert said as he closed the door behind him and walked down the steps, into the yard, toward the barn. William followed, reluctantly. "Where do you live, young man?"

William looked up at the tall man and mumbled something about living on the other side of Bon Aqua School, and that he had promised his ma that he would be home before supper time. The man looked at William and smiled. "It's a good day for riding. Let's see what Anna's horse thinks about it."

As Mr. Gilbert walked into the barn, he said, "You

can call me John." Moments later he came out leading a horse saying, "This is Smokey."

William recognized him as one of the horses he had seen from his pa's cornfield on that sad July Fourth day when he had chop weeds from the corn.

Anna came running from the cabin, "Thank you, Papa!"

John put the sidesaddle on the horse and helped his daughter position herself as he handed her the leather straps, saying, "Be careful, follow the path to the creek, and be back before sundown." John felt thankful that he had found such a dependable animal for his family.

The big collie ran alongside Anna and William as they rode down the hill. The path curved slightly, and the hill was not as steep as it had seemed when William first rode into the yard.

It was fun riding with the sound of water echoing in their ears. The rays of the sun, dancing through the trees, made the ripples in the water glisten. "Is the cave a part of your papa's land?" William asked.

"Yes, one more curve and the creek will run into it," Anna said as she moved the leather straps so her horse would catch up with William's horse. "Let's tie the horses there," she said as she pointed to a tree with low hanging branches.

"Great idea!" William brought Good Boy to a stop and held onto a limb as he climbed down. He tied his horse and reached for the leather straps Anna was holding. He tied her horse to another limb and helped her down from the sidesaddle.

The big collie sat beside the horses as Anna and William pulled off their shoes and socks and waded into the water.

CHAPTER SEVEN

Exploring the Cave

William had never seen such a large opening in the side of a hill before. The cave was taller than his pa's car, and the water ran into it and went underground about ten feet from the entrance. There were steps on the left side leading up from the water.

"Come on. I'll show you!" Anna said, her voice echoing throughout the area. She held her dress so her clothing wouldn't get wet as they waded through the water. They climbed the steps to the left and felt their way along the wall.

"It's dark in here," William said in a low voice as they entered the first room. He almost wished he had stayed on his horse.

"The second room is better than this one," Anna said, feeling her way along the wall and through the passageway that curved into the second room. Then, holding the tail of her dress close to her knees and bending over, she made her way through the opening while William was feeling his way close behind her.

"Isn't this great!" she exclaimed.

Rounding the corner and reaching the second room, William could not believe his eyes. The rays of the sun shining through the hole in the ceiling made it possible to see the drawings Anna had told him about. He walked along the inner wall of the cave looking at all the Indian art. Then he stood in the middle of the room right under the hole in the ceiling and surveyed the whole wall. He noticed that there were no drawings at the far end. Walking over, he thought he might draw something. He picked up a small rock and, just as he began to mark on the wall, he heard water dripping. "Listen, there's water on the other side. Sounds like there might be another room."

He dropped the rock as he pressed his ear close to where the sound was coming from. Anna walked over to where William was listening.

"You're right!" she said as she held her ear close to the wall. "Sounds like water dripping on the floor. Let's go back and tell Papa. He has a shovel. Maybe he could help us dig through!"

William kept listening.

"William! Come on! Let's hurry. Maybe we can dig through the wall before it gets dark!"

In moments they were outside the cave and wading through the water. After putting their socks and shoes on, they mounted their horses and rode quickly up the hill to Anna's house.

They tied Good Boy and Smoky to the gate post and ran up the steps of the log cabin with Lady close behind.

William stood on the porch patting Lady on the head as Anna ran into the cabin to talk to her mama and papa. She told them about hearing a noise like water dripping on the other side of the wall in the cave.

Her papa got up from the table and walked over to get a drink of water. Then he said, "Maybe we better check this out."

The twins ran to the front door and stood looking at William. "How old are you?" William asked as he walked over to them.

Each one of the boys held up two fingers.

"William!" Anna called.

William walked into the kitchen with the twins following.

"This is Ruth. She's my mama."

"Hi, ma'am."

"Hi, how are you, William?"

"Okay, ma'am. We had fun exploring the cave."

Anna walked over to her little brothers and said "William, this is Matthew, and this is Timothy." William held out his hands to the boys, and they started playing a slapping game with him as Anna's papa walked to the front of the cabin. He stood at the door for a moment and then stepped out onto the front porch.

Anna and William followed him to the barn where he got a shovel and a pick that hung by the barn door. Lady found a spot in the shade for an afternoon nap as Anna poured water into a big bucket for William's horse.

"Let's walk to the cave and give the horses a rest," John said as he positioned the shovel and pick on his shoulder.

Anna and William ran ahead. They got to the cave about five minutes before Anna's papa, and were listening to the sounds through the wall when he came through the opening with the shovel and pick. "You can hear the water dripping here," Anna said, pointing to the place in the corner of the room where there were no drawings.

Her papa walked over and listened. "I believe you're right, there is water dripping!" Motioning for Anna and William to stand aside, he laid the shovel on the ground, swung the pick back over his strong shoulders, and brought it forward with a mighty blow to the wall of the cave. He continued to do this for several minutes until a big pile of red clay lay at his feet. "Look at this," he said pointing to the wall. "Someone pushed this slab of rock into the opening and then put clay around it, blocking the entrance."

Taking a deep breath, he placed both hands on the rock, positioned his fingers on the rock's edge, and pulled as hard as he could. It moved slightly. He pulled again and again until it finally fell to one side. Where the rock had been, there was now an opening.

"It's too dark to see anything," John said, as he looked into what seemed to be a narrow passageway. He sat down and leaned back against the wall of the cave to rest for a moment. "Anna, would you and William go to the house and bring back a lantern. Ask Mama to light it for you. And while you're there, each of you put on a pair of my old ragged overalls so you won't get your clothes dirty. When you come back with the light, we'll crawl through the passage and see where it leads."

The two hurried out of the cave, through the water, and made their way up the hill to the log cabin. They were back in record time with the lantern. William and Anna looked a little funny in John's overalls. The pant legs, worn thin at the knees, had been much too long. So, Ruth had turned them up, making a double thickness, and secured them with big safety pins.

"You two wait here," John said, as he adjusted the wick of the lantern so that the flame gave off a better light. He placed the lantern on the cave floor through the opening and scooted it along as he crawled through the passage with water dripping all around. He moved cautiously, holding the lantern over his head now and then so he would have a better view of what was ahead. After crawling about four feet, John found himself in what looked like another room. It was cold, damp, and water was dripping from the ceiling. He wiped the water from his face with his shirt sleeve and shouted for Anna and William to stay in the second room until he checked things out.

In a few moments, John called to them and they moved quickly through the opening toward the lantern light. "I'm glad I've got on overalls instead of my long dress," Anna whispered as water dripped all around.

"Wow, stalactites and stalagmites," they heard John saying from the third room of the cave.

"What is he talking about?" William asked.

"I don't know, we'll have to wait and see," Anna said, shivering.

CHAPTER EIGHT

An Unexpected Find

Anna and William stood up inside the third room of the cave. "What is it," Anna asked, as she walked toward the lantern light.

"It's beautiful!" William gasped as he touched what looked like a giant icicle hanging from the roof of the cave. "It's wet, and there's something dripping to the floor."

"That's water with calcium carbonate deposits coming down from the ceiling. It's called a stalactite," John said as he touched the end of it.

On the floor of the cave below the stalactite, there was a mound-like formation. Looking down, John said, "This is a stalagmite. It gets taller as calcium carbonate is deposited on the floor of the cave while dripping from the stalactite." John pointed to the long stalactite that tapered down from the ceiling of the cave.

"You sure know a lot of things," William said as he bent over and touched a stalagmite.

"I read a lot," John said, smiling. "There's a lot of interesting and exciting things to learn. There are faraway places and there are caves, rivers, and interesting people to read about here in Bon Aqua. Travelers come from all over the United States to visit Bon Aqua Springs Resort. Did you know that there are seven different natural springs at the resort, and some people stay there all summer enjoying them."

"Wow!" William said. "Have you ever been to the resort?"

"Only in my thoughts while reading. Sometimes that's more fun than actually being there," John said as he sat down beside the lantern to rest a moment.

"Tell us again about stalactites and stalagmites," Anna said as she sat down on the floor beside her papa.

"A stalactite is formed as mineral water, known as calcium carbonate, drips from the top of a cave. As the water drips off the stalactite onto the ground below, it forms a stalagmite on the floor beneath. The two will eventually be joined together as this dripping process continues." John pointed to a stalactite and then to a stalagmite directly under it as he continued. "I'll say it this way, the stalagmite gets taller and taller and eventually, after many years, touches the end of the stalactite that is above it, forming a column. It sounds complicated but it's really very simple."

John got up and carried the lantern over to a stalactite and a stalagmite that had joined together. He showed Anna and William the column that extended from the ceiling down to the floor.

"Wow!" William said as he looked all around. "I've never, ever, seen anything like this before."

"Me either!" said Anna.

"There are a lot of great things in this world to see," John said as he walked over to the far end of the cave.

CHAPTER NINE

The Buried Treasure

Anna, William, and John continued to explore the cave.

"Papa, look here!"

John held the lantern closer to where his daughter was pointing. There, in the shadow, he saw a dry portion of wall that had a rough drawing of an old chest on it.

"It may be a treasure chest," Anna exclaimed. "Maybe something is buried on the ground in front of it."

"I'll go get the pick and shovel," William said as he made his way toward the passageway.

"Wait! I'll carry the lantern, and we'll all crawl back to the sunlight," John cautioned.

The three of them crawled through the damp passageway to the second room of the cave. It felt good to be in the sunlight again. They stood under the hole in the ceiling of the room so the rays of the sun would shine on them. Anna shivered in her damp clothing as she stood there soaking up the warmth.

Putting his arm around his daughter, John said, "Why don't you go tell Mama what we've found, and put on some dry clothes."

"That's a great idea," Anna said, as the thought of crawling back through the passageway made her shudder.

She hurried outside wondering why someone had drawn on the wall inside the third room of a cave and had blocked the passageway. "There's only one answer," she whispered. "The mystery person buried a treasure, marked its location, and planned to return for it."

After wading through the water from the cave, Anna quickly put on her socks and shoes and hurried up the hill. Lady ran to meet her as she walked through the yard. Stopping for a brief moment to catch her breath, Anna gave Lady a pat on the head, then hurried inside the cabin.

"Mama, Mama!" she called.

"I'm in the kitchen," Ruth said.

She was giving Matthew and Timothy home-made cookies from the cookie jar as Anna walked into the room.

"Mama! There's a buried treasure in the cave! I'm positive of it! There's no other explanation!" Anna blurted out.

"Slow down and start from the beginning. But first, go put on some dry clothes. You look like you've crawled through a pile of mud!"

Ruth took the teakettle from the stove and poured hot water into a big wash pan, and then she put in three dippers of cool water from the wood-en bucket. After running her hand through the water and making sure it was not too hot, she carried the pan into Anna's room and sat it on her washstand.

"Mama, this is so exciting," Anna said, as she let the wet overalls drop to the floor. Picking up her dirty clothes, she started to put them in the clothes basket.

"Let me have those," Ruth said. "I'll put them in a tub of water for soaking. They'll come clean much easier that way."

Anna bathed her face and hands in the wash pan. Then, putting the big pan on the floor and standing in it, she continued her bathing. Ruth carried the dirty clothes into the kitchen and put them in a tub of cool water as the twins watched. Then, she gave each of them a small glass of milk and waited while they drank it, making sure none was spilled on the floor. "Let's go rock," she said. They followed her to the rocking chair by the fireplace in the front room.

Anna put on her blue dress, pulled her hair back, and tied it with the same blue ribbon she had worn when William first saw her in the woods. Then she walked into the front room where Ruth was rocking the twins. "Mama, it's so exciting. There's a buried treasure! I'm sure of it! I'll stay here with Mat and Tim while you go down and see what we've found."

"Thank you, Anna. That's very thoughtful of you," Ruth said, as Anna took Mat from her arms and carried him to the cot in the corner by the window. Ruth got up from the rocking chair with Tim and laid him at the other end of the cot. "The boys should sleep a couple of hours," she said, as she hurried into her bedroom to put on the last clean pair of her husband's old worn-out overalls.

"You look funny, Mama, in Papa's pants," Anna said as Ruth came back into the front room.

"They're a little big on me, too," Ruth said as she went out the front door.

Anna rocked back and forth in the rocking chair

feeling that she must be the luckiest person in the world. She had two baby brothers, a good mama and papa, and they were in the process of finding a buried treasure. "And it sure feels good to be in dry clothes," she said softly as she looked down at her light blue dress. She was glad that all of her dresses were made of soft cotton, and she liked them especially because they were floor length with long sleeves and full skirts. The way her mama always made a ribbon to match was very special, too. One day I'll be able to make beautiful dresses, Anna thought as she ran her fingers across the skirt of her long dress. Then her mind drifted back to the buried treasure.

Remembering that she had read something about gold being found in Canada, she got up from the rocking chair, walked into her bedroom, and looked through the stack of newspapers until she found the one that told about gold being found in Bonanza Creek. The headlines read: Gold Found in the Klondike Region of Canada. After reading the article, she noticed that the paper was dated 1896. "Wow, that was nineteen years ago," Anna whispered as she scanned other headlines. "What if gold is buried in the floor of our cave?"

Anna carried a couple of the newspapers into the big front room, pulled the rocking chair next to the window, sat down, and began to read about other things, like Ford cars that were to be made in great quantity. She turned through the paper and saw where the Oldsmobile now had a curved dash, resembling a horseless surrey. She read about the Stanley brothers' car that was able to handle up hill climbs with ease.

"Gold and cars, there's a lot of interesting things in the news," Anna said aloud as she laid the paper aside. Then she rocked gently back and forth until she fell asleep.

Meanwhile, Ruth had reached the cave and was following John as he pulled the pick through the narrow passageway into the third room. William was crawling ahead of them with the lantern. After reaching the third room and standing up, Ruth walked over to the stalactite/stalagmite column and examined it.

"Is this what I think it is?"

"Yes," John said. "The column was formed from mineral water dripping from the ceiling."

Holding the lantern while John and William took turns digging into the floor of the cave, Ruth continued to look around at the strange formations. The light from the lantern cast shadows on the walls of the cave as the digging continued . . . one foot down and nothing . . . two feet down and still nothing.

John studied the drawing on the wall. One corner of the chest pointed down to the left. "Maybe the treasure is buried to the right or to the left instead of in front of the drawing," John said, as he stepped to one side of the hole.

He swung his pick to the left of the drawing and dug. Nothing there. He then started on the right side. About one foot down he struck metal. "There's something here," he said, resting on the handle of the pick.

William could hardly believe his eyes. There it was, a real buried treasure right in front of him.

John gently dug around the metal. Then he lifted the dirt out with his hands. Finally, the object appeared to be free. "Give me a hand, William," he said. He and William tried to lift it from the ground, but it would not budge. John dug an area, straight out from what looked like a chest, and moved to a position where he could swing the pick down under the object. "Move back, so I'll have plenty of room," he told Ruth and William. After working for a few minutes, he was able to move it from the hole to the floor of the cave.

It was definitely a chest, and it was evident that it had been buried for a long time. John tried to open it, but the top would not budge. "Let's take it to the cabin, I'll put oil on the hinges, then maybe it will open."

He put the pick over his shoulder and lifted one side of the chest as William tried to lift the other. "Let me help," Ruth said, as she handed the lantern to William. She took hold of the metal handle, and with all her strength helped John move the chest to the passage-way. They waited there while William crawled through with the lantern and put it on the cave floor at the other end. He then went back, pulled the pick through, and laid it beside the shovel and lantern. He stood up and began to look at the Indian art. The light was streaming through the hole in the ceiling making it easy to see every detail. William studied each drawing, trying to solve the mystery of the message.

Ruth and John slowly made their way through the passage with the chest, and finally were in the room with William.

"It's good to see sunlight again," Ruth said.

William, looking at her, asked, "Can you read the message of the drawings?"

"Yes, they tell of a little girl who was lost in the wilderness. Everyone searched for days. Finally, she was found in this cave."

"Was she alive?"

"Yes, she was saved by the cave, for it was very cold outside."

"Wow, I'm glad she found the cave."

After resting a few minutes, John said, "William, you carry the lantern, and Ruth and I will follow with the chest. We'll leave the pick and shovel in here until I can return for them."

They moved slowly out of the cave, waded through the water, and walked up to the big rock where Anna had first read the newspapers to William. Ruth and John put the chest on the rock and sat down on the trunk of the tree. William sat across from them. "The fresh air is great," Ruth said, as she breathed deeply.

After resting a few minutes, John asked Ruth if she was ready to carry the chest up the hill. "Yes," she said. William glanced at the sun and realized that he would have to hurry in order to be home by supper. He picked up the lantern and started walking along the path. Ruth and John followed with the chest, resting now and then until they reached the cabin.

When they walked into the front room, Anna and the twins were still sleeping.

"Anna, we found the treasure!" Mama said as she and Papa carried the chest to the kitchen table. William set the lantern on the hearth by the fireplace.

Anna was awake in moments, and the four of them gathered around the table. John put oil on all the hinges. Nothing budged. "We may have to let the oil soak in overnight," he said as he put more oil on each hinge.

William was disappointed that he would not be able to see what was inside before going home. But he knew that letting the oil loosen the lid would be much better than breaking it open and possibly damaging the contents.

Ruth poured water from the kettle on the stove into two big wash pans and handed one to William with a clean wash cloth. "Use the front bedroom to change into your clothes," she said, as she walked to the bedroom with William and picked up her dress from the bed. She went into Anna's room with the other pan and bathed. She put on her dress, and within a few minutes all dirty overalls were in the tub by the kitchen washstand.

The twins were awakened by William's leaving. John picked each of them up and walked with William to the barn where his horse was tied. Ruth and Anna walked down the steps of the cabin behind them. They each took one of the twins from John so he could help William mount his horse.

"Thank you, Sir. This has been a fun day."

"Hurry home, so you won't be late for supper. Oh, and don't say anything to anyone about the chest until we decide what to do about it."

"Yes, Sir!" William said as he started up the hill toward the wagon trail.

He waved to Anna and her family as he turned his horse toward home.

CHAPTER TEN

The Secret

As William rode home, he had those good feelings again. But this time, it was different. It was as though he liked everybody in the whole wide world, even his pa. It was almost like he had been with his pa all day. That is, it seemed to him that John was his pa. He whispered to himself, "Maybe if I pretend that John is my pa, I'll always feel good."

William worked hard in the field all week. He wanted so much to ride over to Anna's house and be with her family. He told his ma about the fun they had horseback riding but said nothing about the cave or the chest.

"I'm glad Anna is your friend," Ma said as William helped her prepare green beans at the kitchen table one evening. "Maybe you can visit her again."

That was one of the longest weeks William had ever spent. On Saturday night, after he had eaten his supper, he remembered the newspaper Anna had loaned him. He had forgotten to give it to her. He ran to the dirty clothes basket and there it was, still in his pants' pocket.

He turned up the lamp that was on the table beside his bed, and after pulling his shirt, pants, and shoes off, he propped himself up in bed with his pillow and began to read from the newspaper. He read out loud, slowly, sounding out each word he did not know. Finally, he was able to read the whole article without messing up. The last time he read it through, it was almost like Anna was there with him reading it herself. He fell asleep holding the newspaper. Later, his ma took it from his hands, laid it on the table, blew out the lamp, and returned to the kitchen to finish canning the green beans William had picked for her that day.

Early Sunday morning, William awoke with the sound of his pa backing the 1915 Ford out of the shed. He quickly dressed, folded the newspaper, put it in his pocket, washed his face and hands, ate the warm bowl of oats his ma had prepared, and then sat across the table and talked with her. This was one of those special times when the two of them laughed about funny things that had happened. Ma had just finished telling about the first car she had ever seen, and how some of her friends were afraid of it.

Then William said, "Remember when Pa bought a new clock at the General Store and laid it on top of his car so he could carry the groceries into the kitchen. He forgot about laying it there. The next morning when he backed out of the shed, the clock went flying through the air and landed in the haystack. It was not broken, and it sure was fun to see how fast time flies." William leaned back in his chair and laughed so loud that he woke up Mary. Ma started laughing just watching him. Mary walked into the kitchen to see what was so funny.

"You're up early," Ma said, looking at her. She took a clean cloth from the washstand, dipped it into the pan by the wooden bucket, and bathed Mary's face and hands. Then Ma lifted her to the bench behind the table. "Do you want oatmeal?" she asked.

Mary nodded and scooted down the bench close to William's chair. Turning to him, Ma asked, "Are you still planning to go to Anna's today?"

"Oh, yes."

"I'll help you with the horse when you're ready."

"Ma, I think I'll be able to mount Good Boy by myself," William said as he got up from the table.

"That's fine. Call me if you need help," she said as she placed the bowl of oats on the table in front of Mary. Then she sat down in William's chair.

It was a cool morning on this July day in 1915, and as William Davis rode Good Boy to Anna's house he felt unusually free and happy. The smell of wild flowers drifted through the air, and the trees looked liked they had been bathed with fresh spring water. The slow rain during the night had brought new life to everything that grew along the trail, and the birds were singing as if they were sharing a special song with everyone who could hear.

When Good Boy was halfway across the Big Spring Creek, William pulled him to a halt so he could drink. The sound of the water flowing beneath his feet and the birds singing around him made William think of Anna's creek that ran into the cave. He wondered if this was the same one. Maybe he could follow it all the way to Anna's house. He turned Good Boy to the right and rode the big horse through the water. Good Boy seemed to enjoy stopping now and then to get a cool drink. With the warm rays of the sun shining through the trees and the moisture in the air, William felt he could almost hear the plants growing around him.

It wasn't long until he came to the rocks where he had crossed the creek the first time he visited with Anna. "This is great," he thought. "I'm almost to her house." He continued down the creek until he saw the path that led to where he first heard John milking the cow. He turned Good Boy in that direction and held on while the big horse galloped all the way to the barn.

After tying him to the fence post, William walked toward the cabin. Everything seemed unusually quiet. He knocked on the door four times but no one answered. He sat down on the steps and leaned against the railing. The cabin had ivy growing around it with flowers that Ruth had planted. William listened closely to see if he could hear the creek from where he sat. Suddenly the wind shifted, and the sound of the water met his ears. "Wow," he thought. "This is a pretty place." William drifted off to sleep as the warm sun bathed his face.

He was awakened by wagon wheels and horses' hoofs. It was Anna and her family coming down the wagon trail. He watched as the horses turned onto the path and pulled the wagon into the barn. He felt a little uneasy. What if he were not welcome? His fears melted away as the twins started running toward him. Anna and Ruth walked quickly behind the boys. William got up from where he was sitting, reached into his pocket, and pulled out the newspaper. "Thank you for letting me borrow this," he said as he handed the paper to Anna. Then they followed Ruth and the twins up the steps and stood talking, waiting for John to join them.

John put the horses in the pasture and went back into the barn. With both hands, he picked up the chest and carried it to the porch.

"We opened it last night at Grandma and Grandpa's house," Anna said as her mama opened the front door.

John led the way into the house with the chest and set it on the kitchen table. As he raised the squeaky lid, he said, "It was easy to open after soaking the hinges in oil." Inside the chest was a folded piece of paper. John carefully unfolded it and began to read:

> We left our home in Franklin, Tennessee, on the eve of a big battle between the Union soldiers from the North and the Confederate soldiers in the South. We are on our way to Memphis where our son, David, and his wife and little son live. We will be staying with them until the war is over. If anyone finds this chest before we return, please write Frank Smithson, in care of David Smithson, Route 4, Memphis, Tennessee.
>
> As we rode out of Franklin, we could hear gun shots. I was frightened, but my husband, Frank, was very brave. He guided our two horses through the back roads. Everything went well until

one of our wagon wheels came off,
frightening the horses and causing the
wagon to wreck. There seems to be
no way to repair the wagon so we plan
to go on to Memphis by horseback.
The chest is too heavy to mount on
either of the horses. Hopefully, we'll
be able to pick it up after the war
and return to our home in Franklin.

Sincerely,
Amanda Smithson, Year of Our Lord
1863.

Ruth reached into the drawer of the washstand
and got a tablet. She moved to the table with the
feathered pen and inkwell and began to write while
Anna and her papa showed William the contents of
the chest. John lifted a beautiful old wedding
dress from inside. It was made of silk and lace,
with pearls woven around the neck and sleeves.
A box containing two diamond rings with an
assortment of antique bracelets and broaches was
nestled under the silk and lace. Anna spread the
long wedding dress out on the table while her papa
looked at the jewelry.

William could not believe his eyes. In the
bottom of the chest was a sack made of fishnet
filled with gold pieces. "That's what made the
chest so heavy," he said as he moved closer to the
table.

When Ruth finished writing, she looked at John
and said, "How does this sound?"

Bon Aqua, Tennessee
July, 1915

Dear Mr. Smithson,
    We have found a letter from Amanda
Smithson, dated 1863, telling about
their wagon being wrecked in Bon
Aqua, Tennessee. According to the
letter, she and her husband, Frank,
were on their way to Memphis to stay
with their son, David, until the war
between the States was over.
Please let us hear from you so we
can discuss our findings.

Sincerely,
John Gilbert

"That sounds good," John said, as he took
Ruth's note. He placed it in an envelope addressed
to Mr. David Smithson while saying, "We'll mail
the note and see what happens."

Looking intently at William, John continued,
"Last night, at my parents' house, we read Amanda's
letter and examined the treasure. We decided to
write to this Mr. Smithson that Amanda mentioned
and tell him about her letter. Our family decided not
to tell anyone about the chest for at least three
months. This should give Amanda's relatives time to
contact us." Leaning toward William, John asked,
"Have you told anyone else about finding the chest?"

"No, Sir," William said confidently, feeling good
that he had kept the secret.

"That's fine, my boy," John said as he laid the box of jewelry on top of the gold pieces. "We'll put everything back in the chest and hide it until we hear from Amanda's family. If we have not heard from them within three months, then we'll have to decide what to do with the chest."

William agreed that this was a good idea, and he asked if Anna could go horseback riding.

"Well, let's see what Smoky thinks about it," John said, smiling as he started toward the front door. Anna and William followed him to the barn and poured water for the animals.

As John was putting the sidesaddle on Smoky, his thoughts drifted back to the day when he brought him home. He remembered Ruth telling many wonderful stories about the people who once lived in the great Smoky Mountains of Tennessee. She had grown up there and wanted to name the horse Smoky. So they had named him Smoky, and Ruth and John dreamed of someday riding through the great mountains for which he was named. The horses drank the cool water, snorted a little, and made sounds as though they were communicating. John helped his daughter onto the sidesaddle and then gave William a hand as he mounted Good Boy.

William rode Good Boy down the path toward the creek, while Anna followed close behind on Smoky enjoying the beauty of the day. The tiny drops of water resting on the leaves, left by the gentle rain during the night, sparkled like crystal. The rays of the sun danced through the trees as Anna breathed in the fresh air and felt the moisture on her lips. The rain had transformed the wooded area, bringing it to life with many moving things.

The birds were flitting here and there on the ground. A rabbit ran from behind a rock toward the creek. Tiny frogs were jumping across the path far ahead in front of Smoky. The water rippling over the rocks in the creek sounded unusually pleasant, and the birds singing in the trees filled the wooded area with melodious sounds. Anna leaned against Smoky to avoid brushing her head on a tree limb and felt herself becoming a part of the beauty that surrounded her.

Anna and William rode their horses into the water and continued downstream until they got to the cave. Then they went through the wooded area until the creek resurfaced. The horses began to wade again, and Anna and William had a fun time as Smoky and Good Boy splashed around in the water, kicking up their heels now and then. Anna's dress began to get wet, so William led Good Boy to the side of the stream with Anna following on Smoky. He dismounted and tied the horses and then helped her down from the sidesaddle. She sat down on a big rock and leaned against a tree while William took off his shoes and socks, rolled up his pant legs, and waded into deeper water.

"This would be a good place to swim," he said looking back at Anna. "I think I'll try it." With a big splash he dove into the water head first. He splashed around for several minutes. Smoky and Good Boy looked at him like they thought he had lost his mind. Then they shook themselves really well, sending drops of water flying through the air.

Anna listened to the birds singing and watched a humming bird suspended in midair drawing nectar from the wild flowers. The hypnotic movement of the tiny bird made her a little drowsy, and she almost fell asleep in the warm sun that found its way through the leaves of the trees.

She opened her eyes just as William came out of the water dripping from head to toe.

"Wish I had a towel," he said as he walked a few steps down the creek, shaking the water from his clothing as he went. After wringing the water from his pant legs, he walked back to the tree where she sat, put on his socks and shoes, and stood up.

"Another thing I would like to have is a basket-ball," he said, as Anna got up from where she was sitting.

"I have one!"

"You do! Let's get it and go to the school yard and play basketball," he said in one breath as he helped her into the sidesaddle.

"There's a basketball goal behind our cabin," Anna said as she took the leather straps and turned Smoky in the direction of home.

"Let's go there!" they both said at the same time.

They laughed out loud as their eyes met. William mounted Good Boy, and they raced through the wooded area, past the cave, slowing down only when they reached the path that led up the hill to the log cabin.

"Wow!" William said after watching Anna make three goals, one right after the other. "Wish I could play basketball like you."

CHAPTER ELEVEN

A Place by the Chimney

Every Sunday for the rest of the summer, William and Anna enjoyed riding their horses, playing basketball, exploring the creek, and reading from the newspapers she had collected.

One morning before going to Anna's house, William looked through a history book he had hidden away in the bottom of the chest in his bedroom. He remembered being glad that school was out and he would never have to look at that book again.

As he held the book in his hands, it seemed to take on new meaning. He turned to the pages that covered American history and saw a picture of President Abraham Lincoln. He read that Lincoln was born in Kentucky on February 12, 1809, and that he was very poor, working during the day, studying at odd moments, and learning reading, writing, and arithmetic at night by an old oil lamp. William was impressed by the life of this great man as he read about Lincoln becoming the sixteenth president of the United States on March 4, 1861. Learning that Lincoln read many books and became a successful lawyer before becoming president, William felt thankful that he now enjoyed reading. He read for a long time that morning from the little history book and was amazed to find many interesting stories. As he looked at a picture of the war between the North and South during 1863, his thoughts drifted back to Amanda's letter. He remembered how she and Frank left Franklin on their wagon with their life savings just before the big battle.

"Lincoln was president when Frank and Amanda buried the treasure," William whispered to himself. He closed the book as he thought about Amanda and Frank. He wondered why they didn't come back and get the chest when the war was over. He carried his history book to the kitchen and laid it on the table while he ate his breakfast. Ma was busy with the two girls in the bedroom, so he picked up his book and in a loud voice said, "Bye, Ma, I'm going to Anna's. I'll see you and the girls late this afternoon.

"Okay. Have a good day and be careful," she said.

When William got to Anna's, he showed her the paragraphs about President Abraham Lincoln and the stories about the Civil War he had read in the book that morning.

"I know. I've been reading my history book, too," Anna said.

"You've got a book like this? This is the one we used at school."

"Yes, I loved history at Bon Aqua School!" Anna said, and then suddenly put her hands over her mouth as though she had accidentally told a deep secret.

"You've been to Bon Aqua School?" he asked with a puzzled look.

"Yes. I mean No!" Anna jumped up from the table and ran out the back door. William followed and watched as she picked up the basketball and held it very close with her head bowed.

William felt that Anna didn't like him and that maybe he should leave. He started to go, but instead walked over and laid his hand on her shoulder, and said, "I'm sorry if I said something that hurt you." Then he noticed that tears were on her cheeks. He sensed the pain that he had seen in her when she told him she couldn't go to Bon Aqua School because her skin wasn't white. Then he said, "Oh, Anna, I'm so sorry," and he took her hands, allowing the basketball to fall to the ground. Putting his arms around her, they both cried until the pain was gone.

After walking back into the kitchen, Anna took two wash cloths from the washstand and handed one to William. They dampened them and wiped the tears from their eyes. "Wait here," she said, as she turned to go into her bedroom. She came back with a large beige shawl and a history book just like William's. "Mama is asleep on her bed with the twins, and Papa is looking for Indian relics. I'll leave a note and we'll go for a walk." She propped the note against the bowl of apples on the kitchen table, and they picked up their history books and went out the back door.

"I want to take you to a secret hiding place," Anna said. She led the way down the path toward the creek with the shawl folded over her book. William followed, and was surprised that she was going in the direction of the school. She held her dress up slightly as they crossed the creek so it would not get wet. They hurried up the path that led to the schoolhouse. William saw the building at a distance, and it brought back unpleasant memories. He often found it hard to do anything in that school except look out the window and wish that he were somewhere else. That is, that's the way he felt until he met Anna.

He followed her up the path and then took four giant steps so he would be next to her. He noticed how beautiful she was with the pink ribbon in her hair.

Bon Aqua School looked desolate as they walked to the side of the building. William took a deep breath and realized that he felt a little better about the old structure. Anna led him to the window next to the fireplace, and they both looked through the glass into the schoolroom as he heard her saying, "I could always hear everything that was said when the chairs were pulled close to the fireplace, but when the chairs were scattered all around the room it was hard to hear anyone except Miss Lois. I always liked it when she talked about history."

"Papa bought my books, and he and Mama made sure I had warm clothing and plenty to eat in winter as I sat by the chimney. If it were real cold I would stay home and read by the fireplace." She touched the window with both hands and looked through as though, somehow, she was now a part of the class, sitting around the fireplace, enjoying the warmth, and talking about fun things.

Then, Anna motioned for William to follow. She led him to the back of the building. He looked at the pile of hay where he remembered lying as he watched the mother bird gathering grain for her babies. All of that seemed very long ago. He was glad that school was out, and that he was here with Anna.

He watched as she put the long beige shawl she had been carrying around her head. She pulled it down over her shoulders and sat down on the foundation of the chimney. The shawl covered all of her clothing. She leaned back against the building, pulling the straw up next to her until she could not be seen. "You see," she said, "I didn't go to Bon Aqua School, but I learned about history, math, and English in my seat here by the chimney."

William was amazed. He could not tell that she was there. The beige shawl was about the color of the straw so it looked like a stack of hay. But on the other side sat Anna with her history book. The sunlight filtered down between the hay and the chimney, making it possible for Anna to read from her book, and it was easy for her to turn the pages from where she was sitting.

Anna pushed the hay away from her side and looked up at William as she said, "In winter, when there was fire in the fireplace, the rocks in the chimney here next to the wall were warm. I was usually comfortable, but if my feet got cold, I would put them against the warm chimney."

"You're very smart," William said.

"Thank you," Anna said with the timid smile that made her look even more beautiful. "No one knows about my place by the chimney except my grandparents and Mama and Papa."

William put his finger to his lips and said, "I'll keep your secret. What a wonderful secret to have, Anna. I'm glad you shared it with me." He sat down on the foundation of the chimney facing her and laid his history book beside hers. "You know, Anna, I think I could learn better if I could sit here. It was hard for me inside the schoolhouse."

Anna and William talked and read to each other from their history books that afternoon as they sat by the chimney. After reading about slavery and how it was started and how terrible it was in some of the states, William turned to near the front of the book and read about how the Indians taught the white men survival skills in the New World. They taught them woodcraft, hunting, trapping, and how to protect themselves in the forest. He continued to read about how the Indians knew where the salt licks were. They knew the shortest distances between streams, the easiest trails through forests and over mountains, and the most beautiful village sites. Then he read where the white man changed the carrying places into canals, the trails into turnpikes and railroads, and the village sites into cities.

"This is so sad," William said as he read about how the Indians learned that the new strangers were taking their land away from them, destroying sheltering forests, and killing the game.

"Are all white men bad?" William asked.

"No, Papa said there are good and bad people in all races."

"My Pa is a bad white man," William said. "He treats me the way the white men treat the brown and black people. He makes me work all the time during the summer and won't let me go to the July Fourth Celebration at Bon Aqua Springs Resort. Ma said that people with dark skin can't go to the celebration either. And the bad white men won't let the black, brown, and white children go to school together. There must be a lot of bad white men in this world. I hope I won't be bad when I grow up." William could feel that tightness coming into his throat again.

He laid the history book down and, resting his elbows on the foundation of the chimney, held his face in his hands.

"Don't feel bad," Anna said. "You can't help what your pa does. And you can be any kind of person you want to be when you grow up. My papa is a good man, and he says that we should not feel bad if someone is mean to us. He says that when people are mean there is something wrong with them, and we should never let them make us feel bad. He told me that the sky, the soft rain, the sunshine, the flowers, the tall trees and especially the rivers flowing toward the big oceans give him so much to think about that he doesn't have time to worry about what bad people say to him. He told me that if I thought about good things enough that I would forget all about the bad because the good would push the bad right out of my mind. That's hard to do, though! That's very hard to do. So, if I feel sad and can't think of anything good, I talk to

Papa. I tell him how I feel and he listens. I can tell him everything, and he's still my friend. That's the reason I trust him."

"I can't talk to my pa". William whispered. "He yells a lot. But I can talk to Ma. She listens."

"Does she help you feel better?"

"Yeah. Sometimes I cry when I'm talking to her and then I feel a lot better."

"I know, I feel better after I cry, too."

"Tell me what it was like when you would spend the day by the chimney."

"I would not stay all day. When the younger children had classes, I sometimes went home and came back later. If Miss Lois walked toward the table to ring the bell for recess, I got up, ran from the chimney, deep into the woods, and waited there until everyone went back inside. That's why no one saw me. Papa told me what to do. He fixed the straw and even helped build the chimney. He's the one who suggested making the foundation larger at the bottom. He said he did that so I would have a place to sit and could learn from the teacher. We've kept the secret all these years."

"I promise that I'll keep the secret forever," William said as they reached the creek.

William thought about what Anna told him. He repeated to himself, "If I think about the good things enough, I'll forget about the bad. The good thoughts will push the bad thoughts right out of my mind. If I can't think of anything good, I'll talk to someone I trust." William found himself thinking about many good things as he worked on the farm the next day. That evening he shared with his ma what Anna had told him about thinking good thoughts so the bad ones would go away. But he kept very quiet about the cave, the chest, and Anna's place by the chimney. He felt good keeping secrets with someone as nice as Anna.

William would be in the fifth grade when school started, and he had decided that, since he had learned to read almost as well as Anna, he was going to study and make good grades. He only wished that Anna would be there. The last time he saw her, she said she would not be at her place by the chimney this school year because she had already listened to the eighth grade lessons and had studied the eighth grade books. She said she would continue to study at home until, somehow, she would be able to go to high school somewhere.

The nearest high school was about twelve miles away, and children with dark skin could not go there. William began to feel angry at the thought of Anna not being able to go to the school. Then he remembered what she said about good thoughts driving the bad thoughts away. Good thoughts started coming as he began to think about what a nice person Anna was. He was glad that she was his friend.

CHAPTER TWELVE

A Reason to Weep

It was the middle of August 1915 when Ruth and John received a letter from Lee Smithson. John quickly opened it and began to read as Anna and Ruth listened:

Dear John,

Thank you for taking the time to write concerning finding Amanda's letter. Amanda and Frank were my grandparents. They were on their way to stay with their son David, who is my father, when a wheel came off, wrecking their wagon. They buried their life's savings in an old chest somewhere between here and Franklin, and then they started on horseback toward Memphis. As they were trying to cross the Tennessee River, Amanda's horse was swept downstream and my grandfather, Frank, spent many long hours trying to find his wife but could not even find her horse. The sheriff and many volunteers searched the river and the surrounding area for many days, but Amanda was never found. Hungry, exhausted, and near death, my grandfather made his way to our house in Memphis. He passed away three days later. We feel that he died of a broken heart. Just before he died, he mentioned something about hiding the jewels and gold in a cave.

After the war, my father went to where my grandparents had lived in Franklin, Tennessee. He found that their house and barn had been destroyed during the battle. He was not able to find the treasures my grandfather had mentioned.

My father is now eighty years old and lives with us. He is sure that his parents' life savings consisted of gold pieces along with some jewelry they had inherited. Amanda's letter is very important to him, and it would be great if he could read it for himself. He suggested that I visit you and bring Amanda's letter back. I will be traveling to Nashville in the near future and would like to stop by your place on my way there. I will write you later concerning the approximate time of my arrival.

Thank you again for contacting us about my grandmother's letter.

Sincerely,
Lee Smithson

By the time John finished reading the letter from Mr. Smithson, Anna and her mama were crying. He sat down at the table and wept silently with them. They felt like Amanda and Frank were their friends even though they only knew them through Amanda's letter. And now Amanda's grandson had written telling of their tragic deaths.

Slowly folding the letter, John got up from the table and walked to the front porch. Anna and her mama followed, and the three sat for a long time listening to the sounds of the creek and thinking about Amanda and Frank, who had visited the cave so many years ago.

The following Sunday afternoon, Anna started reading Mr. Smithson's letter to William. With tears in her eyes, she handed the letter to William. By the time he finished reading, he was crying.

"I wish they had stayed in the cave instead of trying to go to Memphis."

"I know," Anna said as she and William got up and walked to the front porch. After a while, they walked down the path to the cave with the feeling that Amanda and Frank were somehow with them.

Two days later, another letter from Lee Smithson was received. John opened it and began to read:

Dear John,

I will be traveling to Nashville to participate in the balloon race during the first week of September 1995. Please send me a map of Bon Aqua, Tennessee, showing the location of your farm and let me know if you know of a reliable person who could drive my Cadillac during the balloon race. I need someone to drive to the location where the race ends and pick me and my assistant up, along with the balloon.

I will be arriving at your farm on Thursday evening and will need a place to spend the night. I'll spend Friday in Bon Aqua so I can talk to the person who will be driving my car during the race. Whoever you select would need to meet with me Friday morning so we can do a practice run. We will participate in the race in Nashville on Saturday and will return to Bon Aqua that evening. I will pay the driver two days wages.

Please let me know as soon as possible whether or not you know of a suitable person who can drive the car. If you are unable to find someone, I'll try to find a driver in Memphis.

Sincerely,
Lee Smithson

Anna was eating an apple at the kitchen table. She walked into the front room when she heard her papa reading.

"William's pa drives a Ford," Anna said as John handed the letter to Ruth.

While Mat and Tim were asleep on the cot, the three of them sat at the kitchen table and discussed the possibilities of getting someone to drive the car. After agreeing that William's pa was a good candidate, John said, "I'll talk to William when he visits Sunday." He folded the letter and placed it under the basket of apples on the kitchen table.

They also talked about a place for Mr. Smithson to spend the night when he arrived in Bon Aqua. Anna said she would sleep on the cot in the front room, and Mr. Smithson could have her room.

"The boys could sleep in the room with us," Ruth said.

John looked concerned. "What if he's white?"

"Oh, I hadn't thought of that," Ruth said.

John dipped the pen into the inkwell and wrote Mr. Smithson and told him that Bon Aqua Springs Resort was a good place to spend the night. He drew a map of Bon Aqua at the bottom of the letter, showing the location of their farm and the location of the resort. He ended the letter by saying:

> I'll let you know if I am unable to find someone to drive the car. If you don't hear from me again, we'll have a driver ready to go to Nashville with you for the balloon race.

P.S.:
We would be honored if you should
decide to spend the night with us.

John folded the letter and put it into an envelope
addressed to Mr. Lee Smithson.

CHAPTER THIRTEEN

A Change of Heart

Sunday Afternoon, one week later:

After horseback riding, playing school in the cave, and talking about Amanda and Frank, Anna and William returned to the log cabin. Ruth and John were sitting on the front porch playing a game of Roll the Ball with Mat and Tim. Lady was asleep in the yard. As Anna and William walked up, Lady barked a little as though she were dreaming. "I guess animals dream, too," William said, as he and Anna joined her family on the porch.

"Your pa drives a Ford, doesn't he, William?" John asked.

"Yes, Sir."

"Do you think he might be interested in driving the car for Mr. Lee Smithson during the balloon race?"

"I don't know," William replied. "I guess I can find out."

"It would be great if he could," Ruth said, smiling at William.

William was quiet for a while and then broke the silence by saying, "You know my pa gets upset and yells at me. Maybe it would be better if you talked to him, John. It's like . . . well it's just that it's hard to talk to my pa when he shouts at me."

"Sometimes people are unkind because they do not feel good about themselves," John said.

"Well, I know my pa can't read very well. When there's something he needs to read, Ma reads it to him."

"I'll be glad to talk to him," John said as he looked intently at William. "I'll try to ride over there on my horse tomorrow. What is your pa's name?"

"Oscar Davis," William said, looking relieved.

In the afternoon of the following day, John walked to the pasture and led Mountain Top to the barn door. He poured water for the horse and then placed the bridal around his neck and the saddle on his back. Ruth and Anna had named him Mountain Top about two years before they named Anna's horse Smoky. Smoky and Mountain Top were a great team. Together they pulled the wagon for Anna's family anywhere they wanted to go.

John stopped for a moment and patted Smoky. Then he mounted Mountain Top and was in deep thought as he rode along the wagon trail toward Oscar Davis's farm. He hoped that the right words would come. He felt that if he could persuade Oscar to drive Mr. Smithson's car, maybe an opportunity would arise for him to pave the way for a better relationship between William and his pa.

When he saw Oscar working in the field, he stopped and tied Mountain Top to a small tree, walked over to where William's pa was picking beans, and introduced himself. It was one of those rare moments when the words spoken were exactly what was needed. He told Oscar about digging up the treasure, and about Lee Smithson needing someone to drive his car during the balloon race in Nashville. While John talked, he helped Oscar pick beans. After a while, the two men walked over to the tree near Mountain Top and sat down in the shade.

"William is a good boy, Oscar. You're blessed to have such a fine son. He's intelligent and caring."

"Oh, yeah. Well, that boy never tells me anything. Always hiding out. It's all I can do to keep him working."

Looking intently at Oscar, John said, "He enjoys reading and seems to understand everything he reads. He likes the newspaper. There's some great reading in those papers. There's a lot about cars. Some go as fast as forty miles an hour. Tell you what, why don't you and William drive over to my place tonight and we'll talk about the race."

"I'll do that," Oscar said, as William walked over to where his pa and John were sitting.

John got up off the ground and held out his hand to William. "Your pa said that the two of you would come to my place tonight to talk about the race."

"Really!" William said, looking at Pa. Oscar nodded his head up and down two times quickly.

John mounted Mountain Top as Oscar and William picked up the basket of green beans and started toward the house. This was the first time William could remember walking beside his pa and feeling good deep down about it.

That good feeling continued through the evening as William road beside his Pa in the 1915 Ford, to John's place.

Ruth and John invited them in as Anna brought extra chairs to place around the kitchen table. Ruth excused herself so she could take care of the twins while Oscar and William sat down with Anna and her papa.

An oil burning lamp on the table cast shadows on the kitchen walls, but it was bright enough for Mr. Smithson's letter to be read.

"Here, read this," John said, as he pulled the letter from under the basket of apples and handed it to William. William read the letter with expression and clarity and started to give it back to him just as John said, "Give the letter to your pa so he can keep it and make plans for the race. You will be able to do it, won't you, Oscar?"

"Yes, I would like to drive the car during the balloon race," Oscar said stiffly.

Anna got up from the table and went to her room and came back with the newspaper that told about the thirty-mile-an-hour car race. She handed it to William and said "Here, take this home with you. Your pa might enjoy the part about the car race. This paper can be yours."

Then John told Oscar about Anna and William finding the third room to the cave and about the chest.

On their way home, William felt a little uncomfortable with his pa, but was comforted by the thought that he was going to drive Mr. Smithson's car during the race. By the time they reached home his little sisters were asleep, so William sat down at the kitchen table with his ma. His pa came in and sat down in the chair next to her. That was the first time William could remember his pa sitting at the table like that unless he was eating.

"Tell us about the buried treasure that was found," Pa said, glancing at William.

William told them all about finding the third room to the cave and about the treasure Amanda and Frank had buried many years ago. He even told them about how Amanda's letter was found in the chest, with the address in Memphis on it, and how Ruth had written to Mr. Smithson concerning finding Amanda's letter. Oscar spoke up, "And now Mr. Lee Smithson is coming to Bon Aqua to get the letter and everything that's in the chest. And then he's going on to Nashville to the big balloon race.

"Oh," William said. "I forgot one thing."

"What's that?" his pa asked.

"The son, that Amanda and Frank were going to stay with during the war, is now eighty years old and lives with his son, Mr. Lee Smithson."

"Would you read Lee's letter again?" William's pa asked as he pulled Mr. Smithson's letter out of his pocket.

As William took the letter, he said, "This is the second one from Mr. Smithson. The first letter told about Amanda's and Frank's deaths."

By the time William had finished reading about Lee needing someone to drive his car during the balloon race, his pa was standing behind him looking over his shoulder.

"William, would you help me while I try to read that letter?" his pa asked as he sat down.

"Yes," William said as he moved closer to Pa. "It's a little like cars. At first they could only go about eight miles an hour, then thirty miles an hour, and it won't be long until they'll be going sixty miles an hour. That's the way reading is. At first it's slow with a lot of stops. Then it gets faster and faster. And it's lots of fun."

"Good night, you two. I'm going to bed," Ma said as she got up and started toward the bedroom. This was a special night for Ma. It made her feel good to see William and his pa spending time together.

William stayed up late that night helping Pa until he was able to read the letter without missing a word.

William asked Pa if he would teach him how to drive the car.

"Yes, son," he said, "You teach me how to read, and when you're a little older I'll teach you how to drive."

William took his pa's hand and squeezed it gently as he said, "Good night, Pa."

Blinking back the tears, Oscar sat on the side of the bed and thought for a long time about his family. When he looked at Sarah who was sleeping peacefully beside him, tears ran down his face. He promised himself that he was going to be a better husband to her and a better pa to their children. He lay in bed thinking about the things William had told him. As he drifted off to sleep late that night, his thoughts were on the balloon race and how much fun it would be if William could share that experience with him.

CHAPTER FOURTEEN

A Reason to Celebrate

The following Sunday afternoon, Anna and William rode Smoky and Good Boy down the hill toward the cave. The horses waded into the water and pranced down the creek, stopping now and then to sniff the air and watch the tiny fish as they swam back and forth in the stream. The cool breeze made it one of those special summer days. The rays of the sun drifted through the trees and warmed their backs as they listened to the sounds around them. There were birds flitting about on the ground, while others were flying from tree to tree as though they had found a special meal hidden among the branches. The sounds of birds singing and the creek rippling through the woods created a sense of excitement.

"Let's tie our horses by the cave and look for Indian relics," William said as he led Good Boy out of the water. Anna followed. They secured the horses to a tree, pulled off their shoes and socks, and waded in the creek. They looked for those special pieces of stone that had been carved by the brave people who lived in the Tennessee hills not so many years before.

After a while they both went into the cave and made their way to the second room to look at the drawings on the wall. The sunlight streamed through the hole in the ceiling of the damp room, making it possible for them to see details of the drawings. With the stone pushed to the side of the opening, the sound of water dripping from the ceiling of the third room echoed throughout. This reminded Anna of the stalactites and stalagmites found when they first crawled through the secret passage. "Wish we had a lantern so we could explore the hidden room again," Anna said as she strained her eyes to see through the darkness in the opening.

"Next time we come, we'll bring a lantern."

"Yes, and we'll wear old clothes so we can crawl through the passageway."

After making plans for their next exploration, they left the cave area, put on their socks and shoes, and rode their horses up the hill toward the cabin. They tied the horses to the gate posts and then sat for a while on the porch. When they listened closely, they could hear the water in the creek rippling through the woods, on its way to the big Piney River.

"I like sitting here on your porch, Anna. It's peaceful, and the flowers smell so good," William said as he heard the screen door open behind them.

Ruth, John, and the twins walked out of the cabin and onto the porch.

Ruth handed William an envelope while saying, "This is a note to your pa asking him to bring you with him when he comes to our house Friday. We thought you might enjoy seeing Mr. Lee Smithson's balloon while your pa talks with him about driving the car during the balloon race."

"Thank you, Ma'am," William said, putting the note in his pocket.

"Hope you can come!" John said as he picked up the twins.

"Me, too!" William exclaimed. He and Anna got up and walked to the barn where Good Boy and Smoky were standing. William untied Good Boy and mounted him. Turning toward Anna, he said, "It's so much fun horseback riding with you. This has been the best summer of my whole life!"

"I know. Finding the hidden treasure was the most fun of all."

They waved to each other as he turned Good Boy toward home.

William's ma read the invitation and said, "Oh, that would be fun, William. I sure hope you can go." She gave him a little hug, then turned and walked to the back porch where his pa was sitting in the big green chair reading the newspaper.

Instead of leaving home early on Sunday mornings the way he once did, Oscar now stayed home. He was surprised to find that he really enjoyed it. He often sat in the big chair with William's history book or the newspaper, reading until he fell asleep. He especially liked stories about the car races.

Sarah walked over and sat down in the swing, and Oscar got up from his chair and sat down beside her. She handed him the note and waited silently.

After reading it, he put his arm around his wife and said, "I don't see any reason why he can't go." Then he pulled her close, kissed her gently on the cheek, and said, "I love you, Sarah."

There was early morning activity on this special Friday at William Davis's home. Ma was the first one up. She had breakfast on the table for her family when they came into the kitchen. William and his pa were fully dressed in the clothes they were going to wear to Anna's house, while the girls had breakfast in their nightgowns.

The mood was great. It was fun sitting around the table talking while they ate. Hot biscuits, ham, eggs, sweet-milk gravy, and strawberry preserves were enjoyed by the whole family. After breakfast, William and his pa washed the dishes while Ma put clean cotton dresses on the girls. The dress Sarah selected for herself was one that she knew Oscar liked. She spent a few extra minutes in front of the mirror making sure that she looked her best.

They all followed Oscar out the back door. He carried Rose in his arms, and William held Mary's hand as they walked into the yard. Oscar stood two-year-old Rose beside her ma. He kissed each of the girls on the cheek, then gave Ma a hug and walked into the shed to crank the car. After getting it started, he backed the Ford out. Ma picked up Rose and held Mary's hand as William got in the front seat next to Pa. As Oscar drove out of the driveway, he and William waved to Ma and the girls.

William remembered how he used to wish that his pa would be good to them the way Anna's papa was to his family. All of that seemed such a long time ago. Now he loved his pa, and he knew that his pa loved him. It sure was good seeing him give Ma that little hug. He did that a lot now.

William felt good riding in the front seat beside him. It was especially fun when they drove the car through the Big Spring Creek. The water came up to the running board and Pa had to pull down into low gear in order to get to the other side. William glanced back at the trail of water that the wheels left on the wagon trail. He laughed at the thought of a wagon trail turning into a car trail.

The Ford made its way up the hill to the ridge. Pa exclaimed in a loud voice, "Look! It's Mr. Smithson's hot-air balloon!" The top was down on the car so Pa stopped, and the two sat there in the middle of the wagon trail and gazed into the sky. It was a sight to behold—the most beautiful thing William had ever seen. It looked like a giant pear, upside down, with yellow, red, green, and blue colors. It floated far to the right above the tree tops. It seemed to be about where Anna lived. There appeared to be people in a basket under the balloon, but it was too far away to tell who they were.

"Oh, I hope I can ride in it!" William said as he shielded his eyes from the sun.

Pa got out of the car and cranked it until it started. Then he got in quickly, and they made their way down the hill toward the log cabin.

William kept watching the balloon while Pa guided the car, glancing up now and then until he brought the Ford to a stop behind Lee Smithson's Cadillac. Anna and the twins were sitting on the porch watching the giant balloon. The boys were waving to their parents and Mr. Smithson, who were in the basket.

"Isn't this exciting!" Anna shouted as William and his pa got out of the Ford.

"It sure is!" William said while walking over and sitting down on the edge of the porch beside her. He noticed that the basket under the balloon had a very long rope tied to it. The rope extended all the way down to the bumper of Mr. Smithson's Cadillac.

"That rope is to keep those in the basket from floating away. And the trailer behind the Cadillac is what Mr. Smithson carries the balloon in. That's the car your pa will be driving during the balloon race."

Anna was entranced by it all. The rays of the sun were dancing across the balloon with such brilliance that when she closed her eyes she could still see the colors. She leaned back on the porch and took a deep breath. "This is the most fun day of my life," she said softly. "In a few minutes I'll be up there far above the trees."

Mat and Tim were watching the balloon as if they were wondering where their mama and papa were going.

Oscar was still standing in the yard. As the balloon floated downward, he walked over to the porch to make way for the landing.

After Mr. Smithson helped Ruth and John out of the basket and onto the ground, John introduced him to William and Oscar. After a warm greeting, Mr. Smithson turned to William and said, "I'm thankful that you and Anna found the chest containing my grandmother's letter. My father, David, is going to be very happy when he sees the chest. My grandparents were on their way to stay with him when their wagon broke down."

Mr. Smithson shook Oscar's hand again and

said, "I'm glad you're driving the car during the balloon race. It's great to have a good man behind the wheel. John has agreed to help me pilot the balloon from the basket, and we're going to take a ride today so both of you will be prepared for the race tomorrow."

Anna went into the cabin for a moment and came back with two gold pieces. She walked over to William and whispered, "When Mr. Smithson got here last night, we gave him the chest. He read Amanda's letter, looked at the wedding dress, and all the jewelry. Then he counted out twenty gold pieces from the chest and gave them to Mama and Papa for writing him about Amanda's letter and for protecting Amanda and Frank's treasure. Papa told Mr. Smithson about you and me finding the hidden room and that's when Mr. Smithson gave me four gold pieces, saying that two were for me and these two are for you, William. They're worth about one hundred dollars each."

"Wow!" William said as he held the gold in his hands.

Mr. Smithson called for the two of them to come for a ride. Anna ran ahead and was in the basket as William walked toward the balloon looking at the gold. Putting a nugget in each pocket, he said, "Thank you, Mr. Smithson. The gold pieces are really special."

"I'm thankful I had them to give, William. If you and Anna hadn't found the chest, none of us would have gold."

After helping William into the basket, Mr. Smithson and John climbed in. The two men made a good team. John had an excellent memory and was able to master every task as they prepared for their ascent into the sky.

After untying the rope that connected the balloon to the Cadillac, Oscar started the car and began to follow.

Anna and William waved to Ruth and the twins as they rose high above the cabin. Then they turned and waved to Oscar as he drove the Cadillac on the wagon trail far below. Anna whispered to William, "Mr. Smithson has asked Papa if he would help him in all of his balloon races. He has three each year. There's one in Richmond, one in New Orleans, and then the one in Nashville."

"That's great, Anna! Hope my pa can work for him! Then maybe we could go with them."

"Oh, that would be fun! Papa said he was going to buy a Ford with some of the gold Mr. Smithson gave him so our whole family could travel." Anna and William looked far below as the balloon floated higher.

"This is so exciting! Now we know what the birds see," Anna said as she and William surveyed the hills and valleys.

"Look! There's the creek and the entrance to the cave."

"And way over there is my house." William said while pointing. "I hope Ma and my little sisters can see us." Then, thinking he saw them, he shouted, "Mary, Rose, Ma. Ma, I'm up here. Can you see me?"

Mr. Smithson glanced at William and said, "I

don't believe they can tell who we are, any more than we can tell, for sure, who they are. They're too far away."

"Look straight down," Anna said, pointing, "There's your pa in Mr. Smithson's Cadillac."

William felt a sense of pride as he watched Oscar following the balloon far below. Then he whispered to Anna, "My pa has been good to us ever since your papa talked to him about driving in the balloon race. I don't know what all your papa told him, but he's changing. He doesn't yell as much and he stays home with us a lot. Ma said that he is more like he was when she first met him. Maybe those people who won't let you go to Bon Aqua School will change. I sure hope they will. It's a bad thing they've done."

"I know," Anna said. "Mr. Smithson told Papa that he and others are working together so that all people will be treated equally. He's sleeping at our house tonight. It's the first time a white man has ever stayed with us."

As Anna and William talked, Mr. Smithson turned the burner down to allow the balloon to float closer to the landscape. Then they saw two men and a woman standing near the General Store with angry faces. They were shaking their heads and pointing their fingers as though they did not approve. The three people reminded Anna of a poem she had learned from her papa. She softly spoke the words as they floated above the tree tops:
"Angry faces, pointing fingers, exuding pain,
The pain that comes with guilt and shame
And carrying hatred all through life.
Behind that face there is great strife."

Anna looked at the trio and wondered why they would be so angry at the balloon when there was so much beauty around them. As William watched their twisted faces, he thought about the pain he felt when his pa hit his ma. He remembered how embarrassed he was when he could not read at Bon Aqua School. Then he looked out over his pa's cornfield far to their right. It was almost like he could see himself hiding on that July Fourth day when he had to chop weeds. His thoughts turned to the history book and all the people who had been mistreated, like the Indians, the slaves, and President Lincoln who was shot and killed. Tears welled up as he thought of Amanda and Frank dying while trying to get to a safe place. His throat tightened as he considered the fact that Anna could not go to school or to any neighborhood gathering because her skin wasn't white.

Anna continued speaking softly:

"May we reach out from day to day
To all who walk that selfish way,
Reach out in love so we won't hide
The beauty that lives deep inside.
This we must do for those who died!"

As William listened to Anna, he remembered what she had said about good thoughts driving out the bad. While wiping away the tears, he took a deep breath and promised himself that he would always try to think good thoughts. And, if good thoughts wouldn't come, he would find someone he trusted and tell them how he felt.

After a few moments, Anna and William heard John saying, "It sure is peaceful here above the world. I'm looking forward to tomorrow. I've got a feeling that we might just win that race."

While looking up at the radiant colors, Mr. Smithson answered, "This balloon is my favorite, John, especially when the sun glistens through the silk. It's sturdy. It's fast. You're right. We might just win that race."

They glanced below as Bon Aqua Springs Resort came into view. It was the most colorful valley one could imagine with two lovely buildings bedecked with gazebos and spacious balconies. Cascading springs of water flowed from the surrounding hills. Ladies in their long dresses walked through gardens, escorted by men dressed in their finest.

"That's got to be the most beautiful place on earth," John said as they looked below.

"Papa, didn't you say that Bon Aqua means good water?"

"Yes, and if those springs taste as good as they look, there's great water down there."

"Wish we could stay up here forever," William said longingly.

"We can. Every time we think about being up here, it will seem that we're here again. This can be a good thought that will push the bad thoughts right out of our minds," Anna said confidently.

Anna and William looked up inside the big balloon. Their spirits soared with excitement and wonder as they watched the rays of the sun glistening through the threads of silk. They were in awe as the colors of red, yellow, green, and blue reflected all around them.

Glancing below, Anna exclaimed, "Look! The ladies are waving from the balconies. And the children are running into the yard. The hats, the men in the gardens are throwing their hats, and the women are waving handkerchiefs. They're celebrating because of the balloon!"

"That's probably because this is the first time they've seen one," John said as he and Mr. Smithson looked below.

Anna and William waved to the people. She was radiant in her pink dress with the matching ribbon, and William looked good in the black pants and white shirt his pa had bought for him the day before. He raised up on his toes so he would be as tall as Anna. Standing there together, they watched the girls and boys running and jumping across the lawn in front of the old hotel. The children were waving and cheering as they followed the colorful balloon above them.

Excitement surged through Anna and William as they watched and listened.

Realizing that the children wanted to ride with them in the balloon, William said compassionately, "I know how they feel, Anna. I always wanted to go to the celebration, but now I know that there are greater things than just celebrating."

He touched her hand as they waved to the children far below on that special day in 1915.

Questions for Thought

1. According to Anna, what is more important than going to a celebration?
   Answer found on Page 33

2. What did Anna's papa tell her about thinking good thoughts?
   Answer found on Page 75

3. What did John say to William concerning people who mistreated others?
   Answer found on Page 85

4. What do you think is the most important thing William learned from Anna?
   One answer is found on Page 99

5. Name some of the unpleasant emotions William overcame by thinking good thoughts.

6. Name some good characteristics that you think William saw in Anna.

7. What do you think William meant when he said, "I always wanted to go to the celebration, but now I know that there are greater things than just celebrating."

ACKNOWLEDGMENTS

In 1998, Stafford Armstead encouraged me to write about my years growing up in the South. My thoughts drifted back to 1946, the year that our family moved from the city to a farm near Bon Aqua, Tennessee. It was a big change for me to live the life of a country girl; not only did I feed the chickens, milk the cow, and work in the garden, but I also attended classes in a one room schoolhouse during a time when segregation was being experienced throughout the South. Having lived through those times, I wanted to share about the hardships inflicted on some Americans as seen through the eyes of a child. While the persons and events in *Secrets of the Cave* are fictional, the problems brought about by segregation are real. THANK YOU, Stafford, for encouraging me to write.

During the process of creating the story of Anna and William, Rose Hall mentioned that it would be great if these two brave young people could experience the excitement of riding in a hot-air balloon. After doing some research and discovering that hot-air balloons were in existence as early as 1783, I decided that this would be a great way for our two main characters to see their world. THANK YOU, Rose, for your unwavering support throughout the years and for bringing this high adventure into *Secrets of the Cave*.

The encouragement given to me during the writing and editing of this book by my husband and children has been a constant source of strength. A big THANK YOU to my husband, Luther, and to all our children–Jeff, Luther III, Cyndi, Windy and Vicki.

There were others who took the time to read the manuscript and follow up with constructive criticism. THANK YOU Paul Phillips, Faye Chellman, Shirley Buckner, Howard and Ruth Jackson, Jim and Sandy Smalley, Caitlin Mann, Don Finto, Lynette Howard, Spydell Davidson, Tommy Davidson, Alra Maddox, Hooper Davidson, Sherry McMilleon, and Michal Lynn, Tara, and Stevie Shumate for your help during this process.

THANK YOU Rosie Moody, for giving me insight into the personalities of some of the characters and for helping with the overall editing during the project. And THANK YOU, Ralph and Karyn Henley, for your guidance while publishing the book.

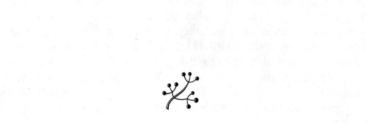